THROUGH ROMAN EYES

Frontispiece: *The* forum *or main square of Rome, as it is today. It was the business and religious centre of the Roman Empire for over 1,000 years.*

THROUGH ROMAN EYES

Roman civilisation in the words of Roman writers

compiled, translated and introduced by
ROGER NICHOLS and KENNETH McLEISH

CAMBRIDGE UNIVERSITY PRESS
CAMBRIDGE
LONDON · NEW YORK · MELBOURNE

Published by the Syndics of the Cambridge University Press
The Pitt Building, Trumpington Street, Cambridge CB2 IRP
Bentley House, 200 Euston Road, London NWI 2DB
32 East 57th Street, New York, NY 10022, USA
296 Beaconsfield Parade, Middle Park, Melbourne 3206, Australia.

Library of Congress catalogue card number: 75-10043

Hard covers ISBN: 0 521 20345 7
Paperback ISBN: 0 521 20944 7

First published 1976

Filmset and printed Offset Litho in Great Britain by
Cox & Wyman Ltd, London, Fakenham and Reading

Book designed by Peter Ducker
Map by Leslie Marshall

Opposite: *A lamp of glazed clay.
The reservoir was filled with scented
oil, and a woollen wick pushed down
each spout.*

Contents

Map of the Roman Empire   viii

1   The Roman mind   1

2   Myth, magic and religion   21

3   Town and country   41

4   At war   63

5   Ordinary people   83

6   The women of Rome   102

7   Mistress of the world   114

Chronological chart   130

Suggestions for further reading   132

List of passages quoted   134

Acknowledgments

Thanks are due to the following for permission to reproduce photographs: Mansell Collection, pp. ii, 1, 2, 3, 5, 7, 12, 15, 16, 17, 19 (right), 21, 25 (photo Alinari–Giraudon), 29, 32, 34 (left), 35 (left), 37, 39, 43, 44, 46, 47, 53, 58, 64, 67, 69, 70, 72, 74, 76, 79, 81, 85, 86, 87, 88, 90, 92, 96, 98, 99, 100, 101, 102, 106, 109, 110, 111 (right), 112, 113 (left), 115, 117, 120, 121, 125 (right), 128 (below); Edwin Smith, pp. v, 49, 51, 136; J. Allan Cash, p. 6; British Library Board, pp. 9, 19 (left), 22, 33 (below), 80, 111 (left), 116, 124, 126, 127, 128 (above); London Museum, pp. 10, 66; Bibliothèque Nationale, Paris, pp. 11, 77 (left); Fototeca Unione, Rome, pp. 13, 23, 42, 45, 54, 60, 61, 107, 118; Foto Mas, Barcelona, p. 20; Macmillan London Ltd, pp. 24, 34 (right) from *An Introduction to the Roman World* by P. D. Arnott; Vatican Library, p. 26; the Louvre, Paris (photos Giraudon), pp. 30, 31, 73, 93, 125 (left); Ny Carlsberg Glyptotek, Copenhagen, p. 33 (above); Guildhall Museum, London, p. 35 (right); Archiv für Kunst und Geschichte, Berlin, p. 36; Ernesto Richter, Rome, p. 38; Ashmolean Museum, Oxford, pp. 56, 57; Alinari, p. 59; Staatliche Antikensammlungen und Glyptothek, Munich, pp. 62, 75, 83; National Museum of Wales, p. 65; Evans Brothers Ltd, London, p. 71, from *Enemy of Rome* by Leonard Cottrell; French Government Tourist Office, p. 77; Weidenfeld & Nicolson Ltd, pp. 78 (Gabinetto Fotografic Nazionale, Rome), 97; Gloucester City Museums, p. 83; Metropolitan Museum of Art, New York, gift of Edward Harkness, 1917–18, p. 84; Landesmuseum, Trier, pp. 91, 108; Hirmer Fotoarchiv, Munich, p. 95; Victoria and Albert Museum, p. 103; Directorate General of Antiquities, Tripoli, p. 104; Kunsthistorisches Museum, Vienna, p. 113; Museo delle Terme, Rome, p. 122; Foto Tadema Sporry, Netherlands, p. 129.

for our children

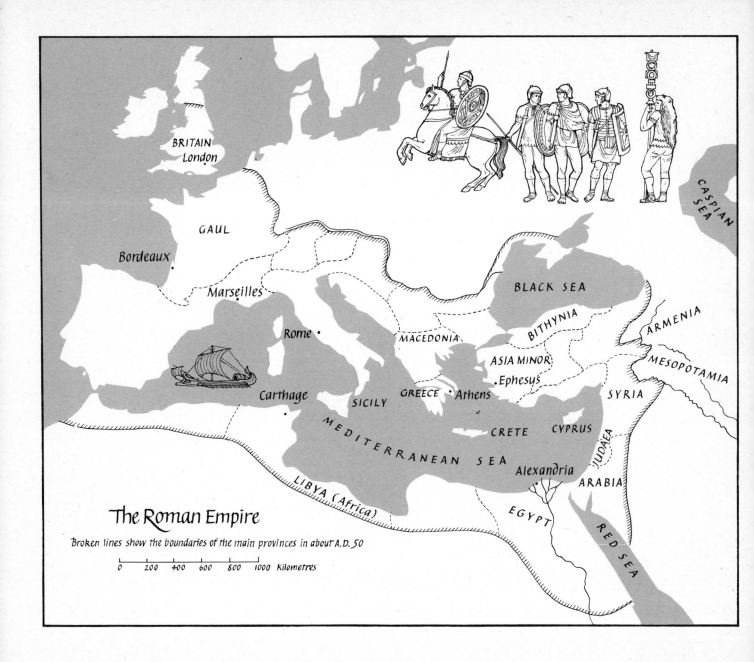

BRITAIN
London

GAUL

Bordeaux

Marseilles

Rome

Carthage

SICILY

MACEDONIA

BLACK SEA

BITHYNIA

ASIA MINOR

Ephesus

GREECE • Athens

CRETE   CYPRUS

MEDITERRANEAN SEA

Alexandria

CASPIAN SEA

ARMENIA

MESOPOTAMIA

SYRIA

JUDAEA

ARABIA

EGYPT

RED SEA

LIBYA (Africa)

The Roman Empire

Broken lines show the boundaries of the main provinces in about A.D. 50

0   200   400   600   800   1000 Kilometres

1 · The Roman mind

In a speech made to the Senate in 63 B.C., Julius Caesar had this to say about the Romans of former times:

Our ancestors, gentlemen, were good at planning, and full of courage in action. They were also without the sort of pride which might otherwise have stopped them imitating whatever was worthwhile in the culture of other nations. For example, they copied the armour and weapons of the Samnites, and their official robes and insignia came on the whole from the Etruscans. In fact, they eagerly imitated any promising idea, whether it came from a friend or an enemy; they preferred to take over what was worthwhile, rather than envy it from a distance.[1]

Samnite soldiers: Rome's earliest enemies, and some of her fiercest.

A Roman nobleman, possibly sacrificing. His formal clothing and the ritual position of his hands were imitated by the Romans from the Italian tribes they conquered.

Caesar's words are typical of the way many Romans saw themselves: better at practical matters than abstract ones, better at *doing* than *thinking*. Another writer points out how much of their culture was imitated from the Greeks (something he doesn't entirely approve of):

If in Greek literature the best is always
The oldest, there's hardly any point
Putting Roman writers in the scales at all –
It would be like comparing olives and nuts.
You might as well give up, and say, 'We paint,
Make music, even *wrestle* better because
The greasy Greeks have taught us how.' In fact,
Although we conquered Greece, *she* conquered *us*:
She brought Art to rustic Rome.[2]

Of course that's an exaggeration; there were many Roman writers and thinkers, scientists and artists. What both quotations imply is that the Romans seldom invented anything new. They were best at taking over other nations' discoveries and fashions, collecting them together and adapting them to suit their own tastes and needs. But the greatest achievements of the Roman mind outside the field of literature were practical, in civil engineering, government, administration and the science of warfare for example.

Even so, the greatest qualities Romans possessed were organisation and single-minded efficiency. Where Greek buildings, for example, impress us by their beauty, Roman architecture impresses by its sheer size and magnificence. This can be seen in the aqueduct at Segovia in Spain (page 6). This stone structure is one of the greatest surviving Roman buildings. It looks too solid and elaborate ever to have been used just for carrying water. (In fact, aqueducts like this so impressed peasants in the Middle Ages that they refused to believe that men had built them, and called them 'Devil's Bridges' instead.) Like Roman law, Roman politics and the Roman army, the architecture of Rome had two purposes: first, to do the job it was designed for, and second, to impress people with the efficiency and grandeur of the men who made it. In the more intellectual fields of philosophy

Dancing at a festival, Greek-style.

and science the Romans, compared with the Greeks, contributed little that was new. In their collection and adaptation of the work of others the best quality was the attention they paid to orderliness and clarity.

In this adapting their greatest asset was the attention they always gave to clearness of expression. Greek thought is often subtly complicated and hard to follow; the Romans tidied it up and made it orderly. There is an example of this here – the contents list of just one section of a scientific work in thirty-seven separate parts:

BOOK XXXI: DRUGS OBTAINABLE FROM WATER-CREATURES

1	Strange facts about waters.
2	The differences between waters.
3–16	266 separate medical points; what waters are good for the eyes, help pregnancy, cure the insane; are good for gallstones, wounds, the unborn embryo, waters that clear up acne, dye wool, paint human skin, induce memory, forgetfulness, sharp perception, sluggishness, a good voice; which waters bring on or slow down drunkenness; can be used instead of oil; which ones are salt or bitter, arise from rocks, cause laughter or tears; which ones are said to cure love.
17	Water still hot 3 days after being drawn from a hot spring.
18–20	Unusual waters; waters in which everything sinks; in which nothing sinks; poisonous waters; poisonous fish; waters that calcify or can be calcified.
21–23	Health-giving waters; impure waters; ways of testing waters.
24–25	The Aqua Marcia; The Virgin Water.
26–29	Water-divining; signs of water; how different earths affect waters; the variation in springs from season to season.
30	An historical account of springs which suddenly appeared or disappeared.
31	Aqueducts.
32–33	How to use medicinal waters, and for what sicknesses; the same for sea-water (29 observations); the 5 advantages of sea-voyages.
34–36	Salt inland lakes, and how to make them; how to produce sea-honey; how to produce fresh-water honey.
37–38	How to counteract the effects of water drunk abroad; 6 drugs obtainable from moss; drugs from different sorts of sand.
39–45	Salt: types, preparation and derivative drugs (204 observations); the importance of salt in history (120 examples); salt-foam; salt-flowers (20 observations); brine (2 observations); fish-sauce (15 observations); pickles (15 observations); the salting of fish (8 observations); the nature of salt itself.
46–47	Soda: types, preparation and remedies (221 observations). Sponges: remedies from and 92 observations.

A water-heater. The decoration shows that it was made for display as well as use.

Total: 924 drugs, accounts and observations.

Authorities: (Romans): M. Varro, Cassius of Parma, Cicero, Mucianus, Caelius, Celsus, Trogus, Ovid, Polybius, Sornatius.

(Foreigners): Callimachus, Ctesias, Eudicus, Theophrastus, Eudoxus, Theopompus, Polyclitus, Iuba, Lycus, Apion, Epigenes, Pelops, Apelles, Democritus, Thrasyllus, Nicander, Menander the playwright, Attalus, Sallustius, Dionysius, Andreas, Niceratus, Hippocrates, Anaxilaus.[3]

That extract is from a collection of *Scientific Researches* by Pliny the Elder. Notice how many authors' work he has made use of: some of them are Roman but most of them are Greek. In other parts of the

A factory-scene: making soap, or perhaps ointment. (A recipe for make-up is given on page 109.)

The aqueduct at Segovia.

same work, which is more like an encyclopaedia than a scientific text, he deals with such differing subjects as: *The Nature of the World* (Book I); *Fish* (Book IX); *Herbal Medicine* (Book XX); and *Stone* (Book XXXVI). Each section is as detailed as the one on waters. And the *Scientific Researches* form only a small part of the author's total writings. His nephew (the lawyer Pliny the Younger) wrote a catalogue of his uncle's works, and an account of his working day – you can find it on pages 8-11 of *this* book.

It was only natural that their interest in order should lead Roman writers to try and sort out some of the mysteries of Greek science. Like the Greeks, they thought that science and philosophy were closely related, and that the study of nature would help men lead better lives. Sometimes this study was hard, and involved much concentration:

You'll need both leisure and intelligence
To follow what I have to say: your mind
Must be free from all distractions. This account,
Drawn up faithfully and carefully, is not meant
For idle minds to glance at, then reject
Uncomprehendingly. I shall reveal
The highest system of heaven and the gods;
I shall relate the origins of things,
The source from which Nature creates, increases,
Nourishes, then finally destroys, dissolving back again . . .[4]

No one would deny that these are great matters, not to be lightly dismissed. But other writers were just as interested in everyday things – cabbage, for example:

Cabbage is the prince of vegetables. It can be eaten cooked or raw.
If you eat it raw, dip it in vinegar. It's marvellous for the digestion, keeps you regular, and after it, your urine can be used in a thousand ways.
If you're going to a dinner-party, and want to eat and drink as much as you like, before you leave eat as much pickled cabbage as you want; then, after the meal, eat another five leaves or so. It will make you feel as if you've eaten nothing at all, and you'll also be able to drink as much as you want.[5]

7

A bee, preserved in a drop of amber:

She lies and glitters in a sunburnt shell –
   Opaque and honey-gold, the sun's own breath.
Her life was hard; she's been rewarded well –
   She might herself have chosen such a death.[6]

Or dinosaurs' bones:

Augustus filled his house at Capri with the huge fossilised remains of sea- and land-monsters, which people call *Giants' Bones* or *Heroes' Weapons*.[7]

What Augustus did with them, nobody knows. Of course, he was an emperor, and so could be only an amateur scientist: he was too busy to spend a lot of time on his hobbies. Only Pliny the Elder seems to have managed to combine a successful political career with a really professional approach to knowledge. Here is his nephew's list of his works:

Throwing Javelins from Horseback (1 volume): a clever and careful piece of writing published when he was in charge of a squadron of cavalry.
The Life of Pomponius Secundus (2 volumes): a memorial tribute to one of his closest friends.
The Wars in Germania (20 volumes): this describes every Roman campaign ever fought in Germania. He began it while serving in the army, and was instructed to do so by the ghost of Drusus Nero, who had died after great success as a commander in the area. The ghost appeared to my uncle in a dream, and gave him the task of seeing that Drusus' achievements were not allowed to lapse into oblivion.
On Rhetoric (3 long volumes divided into 6 books): this describes the training of oratory from birth to perfection.
Correct Speech (8 volumes): this was written towards the end of Nero's tyranny, when it was dangerous to write about more controversial or important matters.
Scientific Researches (37 volumes): a wide-ranging, scholarly piece of work as varied as nature itself.[8]

Pliny's nephew goes on:

*A Roman manuscript of about
A.D. 120. This is part of the report
of an army officer dictated to a
professional secretary. Compare the
script with the later manuscript on
page 11.*

Two sorts of inkwell; sealing wax; pens; the wooden frame for wax tablets; a piece of soft wood used to practise lettering

You may wonder how such a busy man could produce so many books, and many on such difficult subjects. You'd be even more astonished if you knew that in between times he was also a practising barrister, that he was fifty-five when he died, and that after he retired from the bar, he was distracted and burdened by important official positions and his membership of the emperor's council. He was a highly intelligent man, with great powers of concentration, and needed very little sleep.

Each year, from 23 August onwards, he began work while it was still dark. This wasn't out of superstition, but simply in order to get more done. Throughout the winter he got up usually at midnight, sometimes at 1 a.m., and never later than 2 a.m. He could fall asleep at will; he often took a cat-nap while reading, then woke up and went straight back to work.

Before dawn each day he used to visit the emperor Vespasian (who also stayed awake all night), and then went straight to perform the duties he'd been given. When he got home again, he spent the rest of the day studying. He had lunch at midday, the sort of light, easily-digestible food people used to eat in the old days. Then, in summer, if he had no callers, he relaxed in the sun while a book was read to him; he made notes on it and copied out extracts. (He did this with every book he read, and often used to say that even the worst-written book had *something* of value in it.)

This late manuscript (ninth century A.D.*) shows the kind of script perfected in Roman times, and imitated by handwriting reformers in our own century. (The page shown is the first page of Ovid's* Heroides *VII.)*

After his sunbathe he often took a cold bath, then had a light meal and a short rest. After that, as fresh as though it was a new day, he would work through till dinner-time. A book was read to him during the meal, and he used to take notes at great speed as he ate. In summer he finished dinner before dusk, in winter as soon as it was dark. This was an unbreakable rule.

It was because of all this hard work that he finished so many books. When he died he left me 160 additional volumes of extracts, written in tiny writing on both sides of the paper, so that the number is really much more than this.[9]

The education of a Roman boy, from the cradle to the age of about ten.

The catalogue of his works shows that Pliny the Elder was as interested in 'abstract' matters as in practical science. Other writers deal with matters closer to the Roman people's heart: government, the geography and sociology of foreign nations, the way to rule conquered peoples, and the biographies of the men who conquered them.

For people to have orderly minds, it was necessary to start young. The education of a Roman citizen was a matter of great importance, and it is described and discussed by many writers. This, for example, is definitely *not* the way to begin:

Nowadays, as soon as our children are born we hand them over to some silly Greek maidservant, who may have one of the male slaves to help her – but not one specially chosen, unless it's because he's the cheapest, and least able to do any proper job. These slaves fill our children's impressionable ears with all sorts of nonsensical legends; no one in the house cares at all what they do or say in front of their young masters. And that's not all: parents make no effort to train their children in honesty and honour – it's all easy-going answering-back, which quickly degenerates into impudence, a lack of respect both for oneself and other people. I would almost go so far as to say that the particular and unique vices of Rome are learned in

Boys at school (top) *and exercising* (bottom).

the mother's womb: love of actors, gladiators and jockeys, for example. How can a mind preoccupied and obsessed with this sort of thing ever make room or time for anything more respectable?[10]

Moral discipline is essential for good education. Another writer feels that 'speaking properly' is equally important:

The most important thing is to see that the child's nursemaids speak well. Chrysippus says that ideally they should be educated in philosophy; if that isn't possible, you should make every effort to get girls of really good quality. Of course the first necessity is good character – but next comes correctness of speech. For the nurses are the first people a child hears, and theirs are the first words he will try to imitate.[11]

After his nurse, the next stage in a rich child's education was school. (Poor children, of course, had little or no education: the most they could hope for was to be apprenticed to a skilled craftsman, or win some rich man's favour and have their education provided at his expense.) Sometimes poorer people clubbed together and hired a schoolmaster for their sons, as this letter shows:

Recently, while I was on my country estates, in my own native area, I was visited by the young son of an acquaintance there. 'Are you still at school?' I asked him.

'Yes,' he said.

'Where?'

'Milan.'

'But why not here?'

To this his father (who had brought the boy) replied, 'Because we have no schoolmasters here.'

'Why ever not?' I said. 'Surely you parents (and there happened to be a whole group of fathers there) would find it very much to your advantage to have your children educated here. Where could they spend their time more pleasantly than in their own part of the country? Where would they be better looked after than under the eyes of their own parents? Where would they cost less to keep than at home? Look at all the money you're spending now on journey-money and the expense of living somewhere else (and living somewhere else is *always* expensive!): why not collect all that and add it to the salary you could offer some local schoolmasters?

'As you know, I have no children of my own; but for the sake of this community (which is like a daughter or other close relative to me) I'm prepared to add a third as much again as you collect . . . So get together and start searching – let me encourage you by saying that I'd like my own contribution to be as large as possible. There's no better present you can give your children or your neighbourhood. They were born here; let them be educated here, and so learn from infancy to love their native town and stay here. Make sure you hire teachers so good that people will flock here from the whole area, and other people's children will come *here* to be educated, just as yours now go somewhere else.'[12]

Boys at 'secondary school'. Small classes and intensive methods were used.

Lofty sentiments – and no doubt most schoolteachers lived up to their employers' expectations. But conditions could be hard, both for teacher and pupil:

Even the most brilliant schoolmaster never gets the salary he deserves. And even this amount (less than any professor gets) is whittled away by the pupil's attendant slave, the greedy swine – and the school secretary takes his cut too. You come in the same class as some door-to-door salesman peddling winter clothes, so there's no point in fighting the system, as long as you get *something* for sitting there from early dawn, in conditions which no blacksmith or wool-workers' overseer would tolerate for a moment; as long as you get *something* for living with the stink of the lanterns, one per boy, that cover every Horace and Virgil with soot from cover to cover.

Even then, you usually have to go to court to get the money. And the parents – they really keep you up to the mark: your grammar must be perfect, and you must know history and literature like the back of your hand, so that when they catch you on your way to the baths you can tell them who Anchises' nurse was, the name and birthplace of Anchemolus' stepmother, how long Acestes lived, and how many jars of Sicilian wine he presented to the Trojans. They insist you should 'mould' their boys' character, as though it was made of wax, and you must watch over the whole mob like a father, to stop them getting up to any funny business. 'You do your job', they say, 'and when the end of the year comes you'll be paid – as much as a jockey gets for a single race.'[13]

Commenting on the dullness of the books he read at school, another writer (the Horace mentioned in that extract) says:

The perfect orator, as seen by an Etruscan sculptor.

I don't dislike the works of Livius,
Or want them all destroyed. When I was young
Orbilius (or Flogger, as we called him)
Taught us them all by heart. Now, I'm surprised
To find them hailed as masterpieces – high
Unblemished works of near perfection – when
In fact, if one good line or phrase stands out,
It keeps the rest (unjustly) still alive.[14]

The Livius referred to in the first line was a writer called Livius Andronicus, not Livy the historian. His plays and other works were 200 years old by the time Horace was made to learn them.

Children of primary age learned mainly reading, writing and arithmetic. In 'secondary schools' (like the one run by Orbilius) they spent a great deal of time analysing and learning long poems by heart, and reading or making up speeches suitable for the battlefield or the law-courts. In addition, aristocratic boys were usually taught riding, shooting and hunting, on semi-military training-grounds like the Campus Martius in Rome.

But the most important subject for a young aristocrat to study was oratory, the art of public speaking. He was certain, if he made a career in public life, to make many speeches, either in the law-courts, the senate, or before the people of Rome or the armies he commanded. The next quotation, from a textbook on the training of the orator, shows that as well as a gift for speaking, you needed high ideals:

We're training a perfect orator, and no one can be *that* unless he's of good character. That's why we demand not only outstanding ability as a speaker, but also high intellectual and moral standards as well. For I don't agree with those who say it's up to philosophers alone to decide how a good, honest life should be led. The man who wants to be a true citizen, capable of dealing with all matters of public or private importance, of guiding cities with good advice, strengthening them with good laws, or correcting their mistakes with wise judgements – such a man must also be a good orator.

Therefore, although I grant that I make use of principles laid down in

Cicero. A formal statue for the courts or the senate-house.

philosophical textbooks, I do so only because I believe that they're relevant in the training of oratory as well – and therefore relevant to this book. I shall talk very frequently of justice, courage, moderation and other similar qualities; after all, there's hardly a case in the courts which doesn't involve one or other of them. They all need to be defined with care as well as eloquence – and surely this proves that when equal amounts of intellectual force and masterly speaking are needed, the orator is the best person to supply them.[15]

Four centuries earlier, Plato had made a similar point, that the ideal ruler of a state would be a man able to put philosophical principles into practice. Certainly all Roman writers on oratory stress that technique in speaking is not enough without good qualities of character as well. Here is another author's comment:

In the old days people understood this very well, that the objectives of the orator would not be reached merely by declaiming in schools of rhetoric, practising their tongues and voices in made-up arguments that had no contact at all with real life. No: the necessity was to fill their hearts and minds with the qualities needed to discuss good and evil, honour and dishonour, justice and injustice – for these are the matters on which orators must speak.[16]

We don't study oratory in school nowadays. But we learn how to make a case and to persuade, using the written and the spoken word. The Roman orator was trained to use voice and language to move his listeners emotionally as well as to persuade them by his arguments. We generally distrust this kind of oratory when it is used, for instance, by politicians or salesmen. But public speakers still need the same skills; it is now considered more important to present your facts and arguments clearly, but the words used, the way they are spoken and their immediate effect on the audience still play their part.

It takes quite an effort of the imagination for us to see the powerful effect of good Roman oratory. To get some idea, think of the scene there would be in a law-court today if any prosecuting counsel spoke like this:

This admission is all I need, gentlemen; this is where I rest my case – I don't need to go any further, and I can omit everything else. Verres has condemned himself out of his own mouth; it's up to you now to see that he is convicted and punished. You claim, Verres, that you didn't know who Gavius was, but suspected him of being a spy. We won't go into your reasons: you've said enough already to convict yourself.

Gavius said he was a Roman citizen – 'civis Romanus sum'. Now suppose you, Verres, had been arrested and were about to be punished, somewhere at the end of the world – in Persia, say, or in the furthest corner of India – what else would *you* keep shouting but 'civis Romanus sum'? And this phrase would help you, a stranger among strangers, a Roman among barbarian savages in the remotest areas of the world: this hallowed and glorious phrase would protect you. What about Gavius, then? This man was a complete stranger, and you were about to crucify him, when he said 'civis Romanus sum'. Now, you were governing Sicily in the name of the Roman people; should not that phrase, that claim to citizenship, have freed Gavius from his punishment, or at least delayed it a little?

If I spoke of this crime not to Roman citizens, not to friends of our state, not to people who had ever heard of Rome, not to human beings even, but to wild animals – or to go as far as possible, if I went into some barren desert and complained of you to the very rocks and stones, even those dumb, inanimate objects would be moved by the enormity and atrocity of what you did to Gavius.[17]

There is a harshness, an extravagance there, which few judges would permit in court nowadays. But this harshness is very typical of the Romans. It shows itself more in public than in private life, and often comes out as grim, bitter wit. Men in power needed really thick skins. What, for example, can the consuls who dined with the mad emperor Caligula have thought of *this* 'joke'?

At an elegant dinner-party he suddenly collapsed with helpless laughter. The consuls, who were sitting next to him, asked politely what the joke was. 'This,' he said. 'I only need to nod my head, and the pair of you would have your throats cut on the spot!'[18]

When you talked to your enemies or about them, you could be as rude as you liked. Sometimes the rudeness is long drawn out and rhetorical, as in the law-court speech quoted above; at other times

A coin of Caesar's own time. This portrait may be a better likeness than the formal busts and statues that survive.

Right: *Before sentencing Gavius to death, Verres had condemned him to hard labour in these stone quarries, at Syracuse in Sicily.*

it is short and savage, as in this little poem addressed to Julius Caesar:

I won't respect you, Caesar. Can't you see?
Be white or black – it's all the same to me.[19]

Hundreds of poems like that were circulated about the great figures of the day. They were to the Romans what cartoons are to us. Some writers, like Martial, earned their living by writing them. No subject was too ordinary – or too strange – to escape Martial's acid wit. Here are three of his poems – chosen from well over a thousand.

On Paulla

Ah Paulla, courting Priscus? Clever gel!
Oh Priscus, running? You've got sense as well.

To Faustus

You write so many notes 'to lady-friends' –
Now why is that, when none an answer sends?

To Maro

No money now? You've put me in your will?
How are you, dear old Maro? Feeling . . . *ill*?[20]

This relief sculpture is of a small child playing the flute; it is probably part of her tombstone.

This attitude is very typical of the Romans. Even the greatest writers, composing masterpieces on the most elevated of subjects, take no trouble to avoid rhetoric or savage humour. Perhaps it was a way of hiding emotion, of keeping one's real feelings private and personal. A Roman in public was hard and unbending; only at home, with his own family or friends, would he risk as much human warmth as this:

Dear father Fronto, mother Flacilla, take
   Erotion, my sweetheart: love her well.
Let her not tremble at the Stygian Lake
   Or shrink from the jaws of the Hound of Hell.
She would have been six today – a winter day,
   A winter birthday. She died six days ago.
And now, lisping my name, Erotion must play
   While the reverend Dead look on below.
Bruise not her bones, sweet earth, but softly press –
Her feet trod lightly, caused you no distress.[21]

2 · Myth, magic and religion

An Etruscan statue of Mars.

The Romans had nothing to compare with the great treasury of Greek myths. Their own are fewer and more purposeful. Many Greek myths are very complex, and were developed and retold partly because they were enjoyable as stories; some, like that of Proserpina, are based on the workings of nature. But Roman myths are linked with the history of Rome and with her role in the world. They are manufactured, either consciously as propaganda, or unconsciously out of natural feelings of loyalty and solidarity.

The founder of the Roman race was Aeneas, and his descendants ruled after him in the town called Alba Longa. Livy goes on to tell what happened to one of them, King Numitor:

Amulius drove his elder brother, Numitor, out of Alba Longa and seized power. He went even further, killing his brother's sons and making his daughter, Rhea Silvia, a Vestal Virgin; this looked like an honour, but by sentencing her to lifelong virginity, it denied her any hope of children.

But, in my opinion, the foundation of our great city lay in the hands of the fates, and the beginning of our vast empire was due to the protection of the gods. Silvia was raped and gave birth to twins. She declared that their unknown father was Mars – she may really have believed it, or perhaps she felt it was better to pretend that a god was responsible for her disgrace. But no gods or men could protect her and her children from Amulius' cruelty. He had her tied up and cast into prison and gave orders for the boys to be thrown into the Tiber.

The boys were rescued, first by a she-wolf, then by a shepherd who brought them up in his hut. Eventually, they helped restore the throne to their grandfather.

An Etruscan soldier, from the time of Horatius. Compare his armour and weapons with those on page 1.

So Alba Longa returned into the hands of Numitor. Romulus and Remus then decided to found a city on the spot where they had been left to die and where they had been brought up. There was considerable overcrowding among the Albans and Latins and in addition a number of shepherds came forward, convinced that Alba and Lavinium would one day be insignificant beside this new city.

The project got off to a fairly good start, but an unworthy quarrel broke out and disturbed their plans. It was due to that ancient vice, the lust for power. Because they were twins and it was impossible to decide which was the elder, it was decided to leave the decision to the gods who were guardians of that place, as to who should give his name to the city and rule over it. Romulus took up a position on the Palatine hill and Remus on the Aventine, so that they could observe the gods' decision, revealed in the movement of birds.

It is said that the first sign was given to Remus, in the form of six vultures. But no sooner had he claimed this, than Romulus saw twice that number. The supporters of the two brothers each hailed their own candidate as king, claiming either precedence in time or superiority in number of birds. They started to quarrel, and angry fighting broke out, leading to bloodshed in which Remus was killed. A more popular story is that Remus, to poke fun at his brother, jumped over his new walls. Romulus was furious, and shouting, 'This is what will happen to anyone else jumping over my walls', killed him. So Romulus was in sole power and the city was founded and called after him.[1]

If this is not a very edifying story, it does bring home one of the things the Romans feared most: the lust for power and its consequences. In many of these historical myths, duty and bravery are the key virtues:

As the Etruscans advanced, the Roman farmers fled into Rome to save their skins. The city was protected by guards, and, with walls and the Tiber also guarding it, everything seemed secure. But the enemy almost found a way in over the pontoon bridge and only one man prevented them, Horatius Cocles. He was the defence on which the fortune of Rome depended that day.

Horatius happened to have been placed on guard at the bridge, and he saw the Janiculum hill, on the other side of the Tiber, captured by a

The remains of the Ponte Rotto, over the Tiber. Horatius' bridge was simpler, and built of wood.

sudden attack. He also saw the enemy rushing down its nearer slope, chasing a terrified and disordered mob of Romans who had thrown away their weapons. Horatius grabbed them as they came past, stood in their way and appealed to their love of the gods and to their loyalty. 'What's the point of running', he shouted, 'if you don't block the way in? If the Etruscans cross this bridge, there'll soon be more of them on the Palatine and Capitoline hills than on the Janiculum. You must destroy the bridge, cut it down, burn it, anything . . . I'll hold the Etruscans off as best I can.' He then rushed to the far side of the bridge. Among the mass of fleeing bodies he stood out clearly, preparing himself for the coming fight, and the Etruscans stared in disbelief at his incredible courage. But two of those near him, Spurius Lartius and Titus Herminius, both noblemen with fine records, were overcome with shame and joined him for a short time in repelling the first and fiercest attacks. Then the men smashing the bridge began to call them back, as there was very little of it left, and Horatius made them retire to safety.

He turned a furious look on the ranks of the Etruscans and began to

Father Tiber, with Romulus, Remus and the she-wolf. In Tiber's right hand is the horn of plenty, to show how fertile his fields could be.

taunt and insult them, singly and *en masse*. 'Your proud kings treat you like dirt. You've forgotten what freedom is like, or you wouldn't be coming to crush other people's.' For a time they hesitated and looked around to see if anyone else was going to charge. Finally, self-respect got the better of them, and with a shout they all hurled their weapons at their single adversary. His shield protected him from all their attacks and he still stood there firmly on the bridge. They were just starting to use their sheer weight to push him off, when there was a crash of splitting wood, and a shout from the Romans, telling them that the desperate work was done. The Etruscan attack suddenly petered out . . .

Horatius then raised his voice: 'Father Tiber, I pray to your holy name, may your waters receive kindly this soldier and his armour.' So, fully armed, he jumped into the Tiber. Spears flew thick about him, but he swam to his own side unharmed. Everyone in the years to come would know what he had done, incredible though his feat might sound.[2]

Both these stories are told by Livy in his 'History of Rome', an enterprise encouraged by the emperor Augustus, who was trying to rebuild the Romans' morale after the shattering effects of the Civil War, and saw how valuable it could be to remind them of the heroic aspects of their past. Virgil, too, received his support in retelling the myth of Aeneas. Duty again is a key word, and its performance no easier for Aeneas than for Horatius:

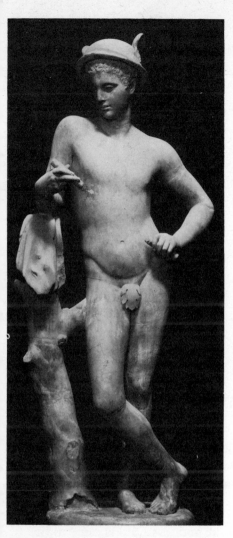

Mercury. This statue gives him a winged helmet, but not winged sandals.

On his winged feet Mercury reached the huts and saw Aeneas building towers and houses, his sword decorated with yellow jasper and a cloak bright with Tyrian purple hanging from his shoulders. This was a gift from wealthy Dido and one that she had made herself, interlacing the fabric with threads of gold. Mercury addressed him without more ado: 'So you are laying the foundations of lofty Carthage and building a fine city for your wife and ruler? Alas! It seems you have forgotten your own kingdom and your own fate. Jupiter, lord of all gods, governor of heaven and earth, has himself sent me down to you from bright Olympus, to bring this message through the swift winds. What plans are these, he asks? What makes you idle your time away on the shores of Africa? If your future fame does not inspire you, if you will not take up the challenge for your own glory, think of your growing son Iulus and of his hopes. The kingdom of Italy and the land of Rome are his by right.' With these words Mercury vanished, and before their sound had died, he was no longer to be seen.

But Aeneas was struck dumb, terrified at what he had seen. His hair stood on end with fear, his voice stuck in his throat. He longed to escape from that beautiful country in his terror at Jupiter's command. But what could he do? What words could he find to calm the anger of the queen?

Dido reacted to the news of his departure with bitterness and fury:

So she spoke. Aeneas obeyed Jupiter's commands, keeping his eyes firmly fixed before him and with a struggle smothering the anguish in his heart. At last he made a brief reply: 'Whatever you can find to say, O Queen, I will admit that I deserve it. I shall never remember you with bitterness, for as long as my memory lasts and life is in these limbs of mine. In this present matter I have few words to say. Do not think that I planned to leave you without an explanation, but neither did I perform the wedding ceremony with you. If the fates allowed me to shape my own life and find my own cure for my sorrows, my first thought would be for Troy and for my own dear family; Priam's high palace would still be standing, and I would have founded a new Troy for those who were conquered. But now the oracles of Apollo have ordered me to conquer Italy. That is my love, and that my country . . . And now the messenger of the Gods, sent by Jupiter himself – by your head and mine, I swear it – has brought his command down through the swift winds. With my own eyes I saw the god, in the clear light of day, come to these walls, and with these ears I heard

Aeneas leaving an angry Dido, from a medieval manuscript of the Aeneid.

his voice. Do not torture us both with your pleas. I am not bound for Italy of my own free will.'[3]

Here duty, to Rome and to the gods, is only another name for religion. Not all myths are as serious as this. The Romans appreciated the Greek myths as much as we do, and the poet Ovid handled them with a light touch:

Now, worn out by her long journeying, the goddess Latona came to the land of Lycia, where the Chimaera dwells. The sun blazed down on the fields and the goddess was parched with thirst; her two children had greedily drunk all the milk from her breasts. Then, far down in one of the valleys, she happened to see a fair-sized lake. By it, the local peasants were gathering bushy osiers and rushes and sedge, such as you often find in marshy ground.

The goddess approached and knelt down to drink the cool water. But the peasants would not let her. She spoke to them: 'Why do you not let me drink? Water is free for everyone to use. Nature has not given water to any one people, any more than she has given the sun or the air. I have come to avail myself of common property. Even so, I now ask you for it on bended knee. I was not intending to wash my body or my tired limbs, just to quench my thirst. My mouth is too dry to go on talking and my throat is parched – I can hardly speak. Water will be like the drink of the gods to me, yes and it will be life; by letting me drink, you will indeed save my life. Think, as well, of these two babies, cradled in my arms. They are holding out their arms to you' – and, as luck would have it, they were doing just that.

This persuasive appeal might well have proved irresistible, but they continued to refuse it and began to threaten what they would do to her if she didn't go elsewhere, and to shout insults at her as well. And that wasn't all. They even began to stir up the waters of the lake with their hands and feet, and out of pure malice they churned up the soft mud from the bottom.

Latona's thirst gave way to anger. No more wasted entreaties, or words beneath a goddess's dignity! She lifted her hands to heaven and cried out: 'Live then for ever in your wretched pond!' Her prayer was answered and they began jumping into the water. Sometimes they submerged completely, sometimes stuck just their heads out of the water or swam around on the surface; or they would sit on the bank only to jump once more into the cool water. Through all this activity their evil tongues kept up the insults. They still tried to spit out their filthy jibes even from under the water, but their voices by now had grown hoarse, and their throats began to swell; and the force of the insults stretched their mouths still wider. Their necks seemed to disappear and their heads sank straight into their shoulders. Their backs turned green and their bellies, which had become the largest part of them, turned white. They leapt about in the muddy pond, transformed – into frogs.[4]

But Ovid was a sophisticated poet, writing at the time of Augustus for a cultured audience. For the first 400 years of her history, Rome was little more than a market town. The area was inhabited by shepherds and farmers, living close to nature and seeing the super-natural everywhere. Everything had a soul – 'Father' Tiber was a god, and you never knew who those frogs really were. Even stones could become symbols of divine power:

Those who wanted to swear by the name of Jupiter would pick up a stone and say: 'If I am telling a lie, may Jupiter save the city and all that is hers, but cast me out, even as I now cast out this stone!'[5]

From here, it was a short step to what we would call magic:

a. The eyes, hands, fingers, arms, nails, hair, head, feet, thigh, belly, buttocks, navel, chest, breasts, neck, mouth, cheeks, teeth, lips, chin, eye, forehead, eyebrows, shoulder blades, shoulders, nerves, bones, marrow, stomach, leg, money, profits and health of Nico, I, Malcio, nail on to this tablet.
b. I call to you, demon, whoever you are and beg of you that from this hour and from this day and from this minute you torture and kill the horses of the green stables and the white stables, that you destroy and smash in pieces the drivers Clarus, Felix, Primulus and Romanus and leave no breath in them.[6]

Strictly speaking, such practices were illegal, but a large number of tablets exist on which the details of death are scratched, in hate and hope. Sometimes the magic was white rather than black:

If you have a dislocated joint, you can put it right again with this spell. Take a green reed about 1·5 metres long, split it down the middle and get two men to hold it on to your hips. Begin to chant: 'motas vaeta daries dardares astataries dissunapiter' and go on until the two halves meet. Wave a knife over them and when the two halves of the reed come together, take the knife and cut the reeds to your right and left. Apply the pieces to the dislocation or fracture, and it will heal. But in the case of dislocation, continue to chant the following every day: 'haut haut haut istasis tarsis ardannabou dannaustra'.[7]

This religion of the countryside and the official, Greek-based religion of Rome worked side by side for centuries, but they hardly affected each other at all. Zeus was renamed Jupiter, Hera Juno and many of the other Greek gods were taken over by the Romans, but they were never worshipped in Rome with the whole-hearted devotion felt by say, the Greeks of 500 B.C.

Sacrifices of animals, in the Greek manner, were the traditional way of getting the attention and support of these official gods, each

*Jupiter, enthroned in majesty. The
signs of the Zodiac surround him;
Atlas supports him. This carving
was probably made for a small local
shrine, or a corner niche in a larger
temple.*

Carved hands covered with magic symbols.

of whom had his own festival in the yearly calendar. But occasionally in times of emergency new ways were tried which had nothing to do with Greek practices:

However, this new idea of introducing Games to calm the gods didn't succeed either in putting an end to men's religious fears or in stopping the ravages of the plague. Far from it, the Games were in full swing when the Tiber overflowed, flooded the Circus and put an end to them. The people were terrified; it was as though the gods had already turned away from them and rejected their overtures of peace. So, with Gnaeus Genucius and Lucius Aemilius Mamercus as consuls for the second time, the general panic was a greater burden even than the prevailing plague. Some of the

Vesta, carrying the sacred torch.

older generation then remembered that a plague had once been halted by the dictator driving a nail into the wall of a temple. The Senate were persuaded to try this and gave orders for a dictator to be appointed to drive in the nail.[8]

We are not told whether it worked!

For the individual Roman, state religion meant very little. To him it was probably just a hotch-potch of formulae and mumbo-jumbo held together by the force of tradition. Even so, there was a strict hierarchy to perform it, from the 'pontifex maximus' downwards, including the Vestal Virgins whose job it was to look after the sacred flame in the temple of the Vesta, goddess of the blazing hearth:

. . . authors tell us that it is not legal for a girl to be chosen if she is less than 6 years old or more than 10; her father and mother must both be alive; she must not have any impediment in her speech or hearing or have anything else wrong with her body; she must not have been freed from her father's control by law . . . and neither of her parents must have been slaves or done manual labour . . . As soon as the Vestal Virgin is taken to the Temple of Vesta and handed over to the pontiffs she immediately passes from the control of her father . . .[9]

With the coming of Augustus and the emperors, things changed. The people had a 'god' whom they could see. Augustus himself was unhappy where emperor-worship might lead to, and kept Jupiter firmly in the picture:

The next night, 31 May, in the Campus Martius by the Tiber, the emperor Caesar Augustus made a burnt offering of nine ewes in the Greek manner, and of nine she-goats in the same way, and prayed as follows: 'O Fates! As it is written in the Sibylline books, let a sacrifice be made to you of nine ewes and nine she-goats, and thereby may the citizens of Rome be blessed with good fortune. I beg and pray you to increase the Roman people in power and glory, in war and in peace, and always guard the name of Rome and give our people perpetual safety, victory and health, keep safe the legions and the state of Rome, be favourable to the Roman people, to the citizens, the board of fifteen, to me, my house and family and accept this sacrifice of nine ewes and nine she-goats which are worthy to be sacrificed. For which purpose, be honoured by the sacrifice of this ewe [here the

Jupiter, with his staff, a thunderbolt and his eagle (also the symbol of Roman power).

animal was slaughtered] and be favourable to the Roman people, the citizens, the board of fifteen, to me, my house and family.'

When the sacrifice was finished, plays were put on that night on a stage, but without auditorium or seats; 110 married women, appointed by the board of fifteen, also held sacred banquets at which they included seats for Juno and Diana. On 1 June, on the Capitol hill, the emperor Caesar Augustus sacrificed a perfect bull to Jupiter the Best and Greatest, and Marcus Agrippa sacrificed another in the same place, and they prayed as follows: 'O Jupiter, the Best and Greatest, as it is written in the Sibylline books, let a sacrifice . . .'[10]

The poet Horace, in his position almost of Poet Laureate, went a little further in his own propaganda, mentioning that Augustus was descended from the goddess of beauty:

Now may success attend Augustus' prayers,
Made with due sacrifice of snow-white bulls
To gods of whom his birth proclaims him one,
Born of fair Venus' and Anchises' line;
All-conquering in war, and yet not harsh
To those he conquers. Earth and sea are struck
With awe to see the majesty of Rome:
Persians, Indians and once-proud Scythians beg
To share our friendship. Now are Trust and Peace
And Self-Respect and Decency returned,
All virtues long-forgotten here in Rome.
The horn of plenty's full. Apollo too,
With shining bow, stands witness to this age,
The Muses' favourite, who by his art
Brings men relief from all the toils of war.
If he looks favourably upon his Roman shrine
And on the fortunes of the Latin race,
Then may he to Augustus blessings send
And of his empire never make an end.[11]

Certainly after his death Augustus was worshipped as a god, not only abroad but at Rome. His successor, Tiberius, reacted sharply to mounting pressure that he should proclaim himself immortal:

Vespasian. 'Good heavens! I really think I'm turning into a god.'

The divine Augustus did not forbid a temple to be put up at Pergamum and dedicated to himself and to the city of Rome. Regarding, as I do, his deeds and words as law, I allowed the same honour to be done to me, and all the more willingly because the Senate was included with me in the dedication. To have allowed this once is pardonable, but to have my statue worshipped all over the provinces with those of the gods would be an act of self-seeking arrogance. In any case, the honour done to Augustus will lose its meaning if widespread flattery gets a hold. As for me, gentlemen of the Senate, I would like to stress to you, and I would like future generations to remember, that I am a human being, that I do human tasks and that I am quite content to be a ruler here on earth.[12]

The next emperor, Caligula, was mad, so we can hardly take the following story as serious evidence about emperor-worship, one way or the other:

Here's an example of his sense of humour. He stood himself next to a statue of Jupiter and asked the tragic actor, Apelles: 'Which of us two is the greater?' Apelles hesitated, so Caligula had him flogged and then commented on what a beautiful voice he had, even when he was screaming.[13]

Claudius, the next emperor, seems to have resisted immortality in his lifetime, but his successor Nero succumbed to it, as to most other temptations (see pages 43–4). The worship of dead emperors continued – unless they had been declared 'of damned memory', like Caligula and Nero. Vespasian on his death-bed commented, with mock surprise:

'Good heavens! I really think I'm turning into a god.'[14]

A lar, 10 cm high, made of bronze. Thousands of these statues have been found all over Europe. This one is from Roman London.

The religious needs of the Romans were satisfied by magic, as we have seen, and by the worship of their own household gods, the *lares* and *penates* who were carried around everywhere the family went. They were the private counterpart of Vesta. Public worship was confined to the 'mystery' religions and to those of Greek origin. Of the 'mystery' religions, which involved initiation ceremonies and secret rites, the most popular by A.D. 100 was that of the Egyptian goddess, Isis:

Above: *Anubis, Egyptian god of the dead.*

Above right: *A garden shrine for the* lares *and* penates, *from Herculaneum.*

If white Io gives the word, your wife will go to the ends of Egypt and fetch water from the sands of Meroe, to be scattered in drops in the temple of Isis . . . Because she believes that she is really hearing the voice of the goddess; as if the gods would spend the night communing with a brain like hers! And so all praise and honour to Anubis, with his dog's head, running round surrounded by a shaven-headed crowd in linen robes and poking fun at their grief over the death of Osiris. Thanks to his tears and well-pondered mutterings, Osiris will forgive them their sins; this is after he's got a nice fat goose inside him, and some sacred cake.[15]

This is the cynical view of an outsider. To the devotee, the whole business was naturally more impressive:

In the middle of the games and entertainments, which wandered everywhere, the procession of the saviour goddess began to move. Women in white robes, rejoicing in all sorts of jewellery and wearing garlands of

Left: *The goddess Isis.*
The rattle in her right hand is
called a sistrum.

Right: *Mithras, or Serapis,*
a Persian god popular with
soldiers.

spring flowers on their heads, scattered petals on the ground in front of
the sacred procession. Others held bright mirrors behind their backs,
which they turned in homage towards the goddess as she came past. Others
were carrying ivory combs and with gestures of their hands and fingers
pretended to dress and comb the goddess's hair. Others again were
sprinkling the streets with drops of various perfumes, including balsam
which smells so delicious.

Apart from all these, there was also a large crowd of men and women
with lamps, flares and wax torches, doing honour with these artificial
lights to Isis, the offspring of the heavenly stars. Then came the sound of
beautiful music on pipes and flutes, and after these came a picked chorus
of young men, dressed in white clothes for this festival, chanting a
delightful song, which had been composed by an excellent poet under the
inspiration of the Muses – a prelude to the more lavish offerings that were
shortly to come. There too came the flute players of mighty Serapis,
blowing along reeds held sideways towards the right ear and playing a

A procession in honour of Isis. The rattle and other sacred objects (including the snake) all had ritual importance.

hymn well-known in Serapis' temple, together with a large number of people shouting and clearing the way for the procession.

At that point crowds came pouring in of those who had been initiated into the sacred mysteries, men and women of all classes and ages, standing out from the rest in their pure white linen robes. The women's hair was oiled and covered in bright cloth, but the men's heads had been completely shaved and their bald pates shone like earthly stars in honour of this great religion. They were shaking rattles made of bronze, silver and even gold, which made a high, clear tinkling noise. Then came the priests, the guardians of the faith. Dressed in white robes that fell to the ground and were gathered at the waist with a belt, they carried the splendid insignia of the most mighty gods.[16]

By contrast, the Greek philosophy called Stoicism appealed to people who wanted peace of mind rather than spiritual ecstasy. It was based on the idea that you should take a detached view of worldly pleasures; 'virtue' was what made men happy:

This life-like head is thought to be that of Seneca as an old man.

Someone complained to Socrates that his travels had done him no good at all and Socrates, so they say, replied: 'Serves you right! You travelled in your own company.' It would certainly be marvellous for some people to get away from themselves! As it is, they cause themselves annoyance, anxiety, demoralisation and fear. Let's say you think money is a good thing: then you will be tortured by poverty and – what is worse – an unreal poverty. However rich you are, you will find someone richer and so regard yourself as so much the poorer. Or perhaps you value holding public office: then you will be upset when somebody is appointed consul – or even re-appointed – and be jealous when you keep seeing someone's name in the state records. You are so gripped by ambition that if you aren't first you'll think you're last. Or perhaps you think death is the worst thing of all: but the only thing bad about death is what comes before it – fear.[17]

The writer of this letter, Seneca, was at one time the tutor of the young emperor Nero. But as the emperor fell more and more under the influence of rich young aristocrats he gave up virtue for pleasure. Seneca retired to the country, but even here he was not out of reach of Nero who suspected him of joining in a plot to kill him. One day he received the emperor's final command:

Quite unmoved, he asked for his will. But the centurion refused, so Seneca turned to his friends and said: 'I am prevented from showing how grateful I am for all you have done for me, but even so I can leave you one thing, indeed the most valuable thing I have, the example of my life. If you remember that, you will win a reputation as noble and accomplished men and that will be the reward for your long friendship.' He talked light-heartedly and also sternly to get them to control their tears. 'Where', he asked, 'have all your philosophic principles gone, which you have been working on all these years, to guide you when things got bad? Nero's cruelty didn't come as a surprise, did it? He'd murdered his mother and his brother. To finish off the list, there was only his master and teacher left.'

He said all this for everyone to hear, but then he embraced his wife and, rather against the grain of what he had been saying, begged her most gently not to grieve too much or too long, but to take comfort in her sorrow from looking back over his life which had been so well spent. She, far from doing this, insisted on dying with him. Seneca did not complain

Nero, as the court sculptor saw him. The blatant absence of flattery in this portrait suggests that it may have been not only honest but posthumous.

of her bravery, indeed he loved her too much to want to leave her behind as a target for Nero's persecution. 'I showed you', he said, 'how you could make your life less hard, but I do not grudge you your choice of an honourable death. I hope we may both die with equal courage, but your death will be the more celebrated.'

Then, with one slash, they both made a cut in their arms, but as Seneca was old and weak from eating very little, and the blood escaped only slowly, he severed the veins in his ankles and at the back of his knees. He was now exhausted by the terrible pain and was afraid that his obvious pain would weaken his wife's determination; he was also afraid that seeing her suffer might make him lose his own self-control, so he persuaded her to go into another bedroom. Even in these last moments of his life his powers of eloquence did not desert him. He asked for his secretaries and dictated to them for some time . . .

As his death was being so slow and so long drawn out, he called his old friend and private doctor, Statius Annaeus, and asked him to fetch the poison which had already been prepared (it was the same poison that the Athenians had used to execute state criminals). It was brought and he drank it, but it had no effect because his arms and legs were already cold and his circulation was too weak to carry the poison round his body. Finally, he was put into a warm bath. He sprinkled water over the slaves nearest to him, saying that this was his final offering to Jupiter the liberator, and was then taken into a vapour bath, where he suffocated. He was cremated without any elaborate ceremonies, following the instructions given in his will; even at the time when he was still an extremely rich and powerful man, he had made these arrangements for the end of his life.[18]

In many of its ideas, such as toleration and the brotherhood of man, Stoicism was quite close to Christianity. At first the religion particularly of women and slaves, Christianity spread more widely during the first three centuries A.D. Christians were not always persecuted, but often they were treated with great brutality:

As for the Christians, the emperor Daia decided to do what he had previously done in the past. He pretended that they would be forgiven and gave orders that the servants of God should not be killed, but then had them mutilated. So the confessors of the faith had their eyes gouged out, their hands amputated, their feet lopped, and their nostrils and ears cut off.[19]

An early Christian mosaic from Ravenna. The quotation from the Bible is 'I am the Way, the Truth and the Life'. The clothing is still very like that of a Roman soldier.

But such revolting atrocities seemed only to increase the power of Christianity, until in A.D. 313 Constantine became the first Christian emperor. Writing about a hundred years later, Augustine draws a parallel between the two forces, Rome and Christianity, which were now inseparably joined:

As far as this mortal life is concerned, which is finished and gone in a few days, what does it matter, to a man who is going to die, what rulers he lives under, as long as they don't force him to commit sacrilege or crime? I do not see what difference it makes to a man's security and good character that some men come out on top and some go under, except for the fatuous pride taken in human glory. That pride is the reward of those who have burned with desire for it and fanned the flames of war.

After all, Roman lands pay tribute, do they not? The Romans don't have exclusive rights, do they, to any knowledge? And are there not many senators abroad who don't even know what Rome looks like? Take away their boasting and what are all men? Just men. Even if, by mistake, the world were to honour some of the more worthy among us, this honour should not be thought of as anything very important. It is mere insubstantial smoke.

But even here, let us make use of what our Lord provides for us. Let us consider what important things those Romans despised, what they put up with, what passions they subdued to win glory among men. This glory was a fitting tribute to their efforts. To keep us humble, let us consider this: that the kingdom in which we have the promise of ruling is as far from Rome as heaven from earth, everlasting life from our momentary joys, true glory from empty praise, the company of angels from that of men, the light of Him who made the sun and the moon from the light of that sun and moon. Consider further then that we, if we are citizens of such a great country, ought not to swell with pride if we do some good works to get there or put up with a number of hardships, considering that the Romans did such great deeds and underwent such hardships for an earthly home that they already possessed. What is more, the forgiveness of sins, which gathers together the citizens into the eternal city, was foreshadowed in the famous asylum of Romulus, when a free pardon for whatever crime was the foundation on which Rome was built.[20]

3 · Town and country

If quiet is essential for working, then I'm doing no good here, with noise on every side. My lodgings are right over a public bath-house, and you can imagine what that means! It's enough to make a man hate his own ears. First there are the strenuous types exercising, swinging lead weights about in their hands, and grunting and groaning whenever they find it hard – or want people to think they do. Their other favourite trick is holding their breath and then letting it out with sharp gasps and whistles. Then there are the less athletic types having a massage – much less high-class. All you hear is the slap of hands on shoulders, cupped or flat, a different noise for each. Next you get a ball-player yelling out his score – could anything be worse? Or else there's a drunk picking a quarrel, a thief caught red-handed, some fellow who likes singing in the bath, or the oafs who dive into the pool with the highest leaps and biggest splashes.

Still, at least all these are natural sounds – not like the hair-plucker, who's always whistling and screeching to make people take notice of him. He's never quiet unless he's working; and *then* he's plucking armpits, and his victim does the yelling for him! Then there are people selling drinks, sausages or pastries, and the men advertising food-shops; each one shouts his wares with his own particular cry . . .

Outside (but just as distracting) there are carriages hurrying past, a carpenter up that street, a blacksmith down this one – and last but not least, the maker of musical instruments down on the corner, always testing his oboes and trumpets, making a terrible noise and never producing a real tune at all.[1]

Roman towns belonged to the masters of the world, the most important people on earth: it's not surprising that they were bustling, raucous and noisy. Day and night, Rome had a traffic problem, even in A.D. 60:

A narrow street: the Via Biberatica from Trajan's Market in Rome.

Opposite: Slaves using a winch to raise a memorial pillar.

How can anyone sleep in lodgings anyway? Let's face it: only the rich sleep in Rome these days. All night wagons rumble through narrow streets, and the language of drivers caught in traffic-jams would wake a deaf-mute or a sea-elephant. A rich man goes to his business appointments by litter: inside he can read, write or sleep – pull down the blinds, and you nod off right away. But asleep or awake, he'll get there first: look at the crowd up ahead of us, the mob behind! We have to walk, dodging elbows, pushed by planks, bashed with barrels, poked with poles – our legs are thick with mud, our toes flattened by other people's feet or stamped on by hobnailed soldiers' boots . . . Look out! Mind that wagon-load of pine-logs up ahead, that cart ferrying a fir-tree over the heads of the crowd. If that load of marble slipped, you'd vanish – squashed to nothing. A leg here, a bone there: no one could fit *that* jigsaw together.[2]

Part of the trouble – and a good deal of the noise – was due to the

constant demolition and rebuilding of the city. At the time of the passage quoted above, things were particularly bad – the emperor Nero (who ruled from A.D. 54 to 68) had an insatiable passion for building:

This was his most extravagant hobby. He built a house extending all the way from the Palatine Hill to the Esquiline, and called it 'The Corridor'. Then, when it burned down, he rebuilt it and called it 'The Golden House'. The following details will give some idea of its size and decoration: in the entrance-hall there was room for a gigantic statue of Nero himself, 38 metres high; the house was so vast that the portico was 3 kilometres long; there was a pool (or rather a sea) surrounded by buildings arranged like a small town, with fields, meadows and vineyards above it, to say nothing of woods and pastures filled with all sorts of animals, both wild and tame. In other parts of the house everything was covered with gold leaf, and studded with precious stones and mother-of-pearl. The dining-rooms all had ceilings of ivory, with small sliding panels and narrow pipes set into them, through which flowers or perfume could be sprinkled over the heads of the diners below. The most important dining-room was circular, with a revolving roof that followed the progress of night and day. The baths were kept full of sea-water or water from mineral springs. When the house was finished (in the same style throughout) Nero moved in, saying approvingly, 'Now at last I can live like a *real* human being!'

In addition to this he began a swimming pool extending from Misenum to Lake Avernus. It was to be covered, and surrounded by porticos; all the hot springs round Baiae were to be diverted to fill it. He also planned a canal from Avernus to Ostia, 160 kilometres long, deep enough for sea-going ships, and wide enough for two huge warships to pass each other. To finish these projects, he wanted prisoners brought to Italy from every jail in the Roman Empire; no condemned man – even a murderer – was to be given any sentence except work on Nero's building-projects.[3]

The Golden House was never finished and the last of these projects didn't come off: Nero ran out of money. It was often said that he was so eager to build that he let nothing and no one stand in his way:

In the course of conversation someone once quoted the Greek line, 'When I am dead, let fire eat up the earth.' 'No', said Nero, 'it should be changed

The monument to the builder Aterius. It shows the Via Sacra in Rome, and includes tombs, a temple of Isis, a triumphal arch, and the Coliseum.

to "*While I'm alive*, let fire eat up the earth."' And he was as good as his word: pretending to be disgusted at the state of the buildings in the Old City, and the narrow winding streets, he set fire to it. He didn't even do this secretly: a number of Privy Councillors caught his servants red-handed on their own property, carrying fuses and pine-torches, but were too afraid of Nero to arrest them. There were some grain-warehouses (built of solid stone) round the Golden House, and Nero badly wanted their sites, so he had them smashed in with siege-weapons, and then set on fire.

The Great Fire lasted for six days and seven nights. The common people fled for safety to the public parks or into the Catacombs. It wasn't only slum apartments that were burnt, but the houses of famous historical figures, hung with the rewards and trophies they had won. Temples from the time of the Kings 600 years before, or dating back 300 years to the Punic or Gallic Wars, were now burnt down: nothing was saved simply because it had historic or touristic importance. Nero himself watched the fire from the Tower of Maecenas. He said he was delighted with the beauty of the flames; then he put on his acting-clothes, and sang every single verse of his own composition *The Fall of Troy*.[4]

That account seems more like gossip than historical truth. In fact Nero seems to have been away from Rome on the night of the fire but came back immediately to organise housing for the people who had

The catacombs. The 'shelves' are for bodies.

lost their homes and afterwards played his part in the rebuilding of the city. Whatever *did* cause the Great Fire of A.D. 64, its long-term effects were certainly nothing but good. Rome was full of magnificent squares and beautiful public buildings; but until the Fire got rid of

Part of the remains of the first storey of Nero's Golden House.

the slums, most of the poorer citizens lived in squalid tenements, jerry-built and always on the brink of collapse:

Most of the city's propped up with planks to stop it collapsing. Your landlord stands in front of cracks that have been there for years and says, 'Sleep well!', although he knows that the house itself may not last the night. I wish I lived where there were no fires, no midnight panics. There you are, asleep in your attic – next to the pigeons' nests, with only tiles between you and the rain. Downstairs, the firebell rang hours ago; the neighbours are shouting for water, moving out their valuables – and nothing but smoke has reached *you* yet. You'll be the last to know – and probably the last to burn.[5]

As the pictures show, some really solid and impressive tenements *were* built – but only after the Great Fire had shown the dangers of wooden ones. Some of the buildings put up after the Fire are still in use today. But not Nero's once-proud palace, the Golden House – as the picture shows.

Building-work apart, there was always plenty going on in Roman

A tenement building in Ostia.

streets and squares: shows, political meetings, parades, religious ceremonies, buying and selling, weddings and divorces. A Roman seeing our life today would be astonished at how much of it goes on indoors.

Not that *their* home-life was always quiet and peaceful – in town, at any rate:

Wherever you go these days, you see more carts in front of city houses than you ever would on the farm. But even that's a treat compared with what it's like when the tradesmen come to collect their money. The clothes-cleaner's there, and the haberdasher, the jeweller, the wool-seller; the man selling lingerie and bridal veils, violet or yellow dye, muffs, shoes smelling of balsam; linen-merchants, shoemakers, cobblers squatting on their heels, men selling slippers and sandals, men who'll dye anything the colour of mallows – everyone's turned up, even belt-makers and girdle-smiths.

At last you think you've got them all paid off, and away they go – but here come hundreds more: weavers, lace-sellers, cabinet-makers, all after their money, standing in the front hall like jugs waiting to be filled. They come in, and you pay up. 'Well', you think, 'that *must* be the lot' – but here come the saffron-dyers, or some damned everlasting nuisance on the scrounge . . .

   With all those unexpected pests out of the way, you're faced finally with a soldier collecting army taxes. You go and sort things out with your banker, while the soldier misses his lunch, he's so keen to be paid. But when you've finished with the banker, you find you owe *him* money too – so the soldier has to try again some other time.[6]

The 'damned everlasting scroungers' referred to in that extract are an important part of Roman life. Not only were rich men surrounded by parasites who made a living from lies and flattery, but almost all classes were involved in a strange ritual, the 'early-morning call'. Every man of importance, the patron, had a group of 'clients' who called on him each morning to pass the time of day, find out if they were needed, and pick up their allowance of money or food.

   Out of this arrangement the patron got a group of followers, eager to vote for him or support him when he appeared in public; he probably also enjoyed the feeling of importance a large group of clients would give him. For some of the 'clients', in a state with no public welfare system, it may well have been the only way to keep alive. But even rich men visited each other: everyone was someone else's client, and was himself a patron with clients of his own. In Chapter 1, page 7, Pliny describes early-morning callers at his country house. In Rome things weren't quite so civilised or dignified:

Now pure-bred citizens fight in the rich man's doorway, eager to get their hands on the food-basket. But he peers closely into your face – he's terrified you're an impostor, giving a false name. You'll get nothing till he's satisfied. He orders the butler to deal with blue-blooded gentlemen first – oh yes, they're fighting on the step with the rest of us. 'The praetor first, then the tribune.' But a freedman is first in the queue. 'Me first', he says. 'I'm not giving up my place, even if I *was* born beside the Euphrates – I won't deny it, and anyway my pierced ears are a giveaway. But I own five shops, and they bring in 400,000 sesterces a year.'[7]

With a testy patron, you had to mind your manners:

The atrium *or main hall of a rich man's villa. Here the clients gathered to greet their patron.*

In greeting my patronus, I forgot
   To call him 'sir', and so he took offence.
And what else did he take, you ask? A lot:
   My casual attitude cost 50 pence.[8]

After your morning calls – and some people had so many patrons they took half the afternoon as well – the rest of the day was your own. Most people had jobs to do: some are mentioned in Chapter 5, and there are pictures on pages 100 and 101. Rich men had business to attend to, meetings of the senate or the emperor's council, or attendances to make in court. The law was a passion with rich Romans: many of them made it their profession, and legal training was an important part of rich children's education. Much Roman law was simple and sensible:

VI The width of a road is 2 metres on the straight and 4 on a bend.

VII Roads must be kept in good repair. If the road is not laid with stones, anyone may drive his beasts where he likes.

IX Branches of trees should be chopped off all round at least 4 metres from the ground (in case the neighbouring field suffers from lack of sunshine). If a tree from the farm next door is bent by the wind over your property, you may take action to have it chopped down.

X If fruit from your tree falls on someone else's property, you may collect it.[9]

But very often cases involved tax or insurance frauds, and were very complicated indeed. If the trial had political overtones, it attracted huge crowds, and could make a lawyer's name overnight. One such case was the prosecution of Verres, ex-governor of Sicily, for extortion. He was prosecuted by Cicero, who went into the most extravagant detail:

Now I'm not asking you where you got those 400 jars of honey or all that Maltese linen or those fifty dining-room couches or all those candle-holders; I repeat, I'm not asking where you got them. What I *am* asking is, 'What did you want them all for?' Let's leave the honey out of it – but all that linen and all those couches – were you proposing to furnish all your friends' wives and their country houses?

All this, gentlemen, is recorded in the accounts for just a few months, so consider the situation over the full period of three years. I claim that from these bits of paper, found among the effects of just one official of the company, you can come to a reasonable conclusion as to the sort of piracy he brought to that province, as to his enormous, widespread, insatiable greed, as to the vast amounts he secured, not only in cash but in securities of the sort I have just mentioned. You shall have the details of these later on.

For the time being, concentrate on this one point. On the exports I've mentioned, it's claimed that the customs company lost 60,000 sesterces,

Storage jars, for honey, wine or grain.

due from the 5 per cent tax on exports from Syracuse. That is, in a few short months, as these sordid, revolting bits of paper inform us, our governor stole and illegally exported goods worth 1,200,000 sesterces from one town alone.[10]

Another extract from this speech is given on page 18. Cicero made his name with this prosecution – and in fact corrupt governors provided a steady source of work for upper-class lawyers through much of Roman history.

Apart from estate-management, politics and law, many noble Romans did some writing. For some writers, the promise of ever-lasting fame was reward enough; others thought differently:

Not only the sophisticated few
  Enjoy my poetry: it's not in vain!
  The soldier on the icy Danube plain
Stiffly picks up my book and thumbs it through.
Even in Britain, they say, men read my verse.
So what? Fame never seems to reach my purse.[11]

Once you'd finished your writing, you gathered a group of friends and clients together, and proudly read them what you'd just produced. A nobleman interested in literature – or with a lot of friends – must have spent many days each year at these recitations. As Pliny rather ruefully says:

The poet-harvest this year is quite incredible – there was hardly a single day in April when *somebody* was not giving a recitation.[12]

However, when it came to his own works, he was hardly the most retiring of authors:

I chose the best time of year for my recitation, July, a month when the law-courts are practically at a standstill. I wanted my works to get used to a cultured audience in their own home, so I called together a group of friends, and sat them down at writing-desks. By pure chance I *had* been called to court that day unexpectedly, to give a legal opinion. I explained this in my opening address, and asked my audience to excuse what must seem like rudeness or carelessness – the fact that I had called some friends together for a recitation, and then been forced to leave for the courts, that is, to attend to the affairs of other friends. 'I have the same priority when I write', I went on. 'I put business before pleasure, seriousness before frivolity. I write first for my friends, second for myself.'
   The book being read was a collection of short poems in different metres. That's how those of us with little confidence in our own skill avoid boring our listeners. The reading took two days: the audience insisted, even though I never leave anything out, as others do – leaving pieces out is like admitting they aren't worth keeping in.[13]

What with recitations, clients, law-courts, meetings and baths, a rich man's day in Rome was very busy indeed. But what did it all *matter*?

It's odd how you can give a coherent – or apparently coherent – account of each separate day spent in Rome, but how difficult it is to account for a group of days strung together. If you ask someone, 'What did you do today?' he'd answer 'I went to a coming-of-age ceremony, an engagement party, a wedding. Someone asked me to witness his will; someone asked my help in a legal matter; I spoke up for someone else in court.' On the actual day, each of these things seemed vital and essential – but if you

A rich family's travelling-coach.

think how many days you've used up in this way, they seem much more trivial. This is particularly true when you're on holiday: you suddenly think, 'My god! What a lot of days I've frittered away on nothing!'

I feel this whenever I visit my estates at Laurentum, to read, write, or just take exercises (for I believe that a healthy mind needs a healthy body). In Laurentum I hear and say nothing I might later regret; no one tells tales about anyone else, and I have no one to complain of – except perhaps myself, when I get stuck with my writing. There's nothing to make me excited or apprehensive, no gossip to get me flustered – in fact I communicate with no one but my books and myself. What a simple, decent life! I love seclusion – no amount of business can replace it! I find the sea and the coast a genuine home of the Muses, always filling me with inspiration and keeping me busy. Why don't *you* try it, Fundanus? Leave the noise, senseless bustle and pointless effort of Rome, take a holiday and do some writing – or if you prefer, do nothing at all. As our friend Atilius said, rather cleverly, 'Better to have nothing to do than to work hard doing nothing.'[14]

Most wealthy Romans – like Pliny, who wrote that letter – owned large country estates, and escaped to them as often as they could. Pliny had several country houses, usually (like this one) set in beautiful countryside:

The country town of Licenza, seen from the villa of the poet Horace.

Imagine an immense amphitheatre, of the size only nature can make. A broad, flat plain is surrounded by hills, whose tops are covered with tall, old trees. There's plenty of hunting, of every kind. Down from the hilltops timber woods follow the line of the slopes, interspersed with stretches of rich, fertile soil – you'd have a job finding any rock at all, however hard you looked. These sloping fields are as fertile as the flattest plain-ground; their harvest ripens later in the year, but is just as abundant. Below them the hillsides are covered with serried ranks of vines in every direction, stretching right down to a sort of fringe of undergrowth at the edge of the plain.

Beyond this are meadows and cornfields, fields that only the largest oxen and heaviest ploughs can turn over; the soil is so clinging that the first furrows churn up huge lumps that take no less than nine ploughings to break up. The grass-meadows are bright with flowers, and produce clover and other grasses so fresh and soft you'd think they'd just that minute grown. All these fields are watered by streams that never run dry – but though there's always water, there are no bogs or swamps, for the land slopes, and whatever water it can't absorb is drained off into the river Tiber. This flows right through the valley, wide and deep enough for ships, at any rate in winter and spring, when it takes all my farm-produce into the heart of Rome; in summer the water-level falls, and the trickle that's left is ashamed to call itself a proper river until it fills up again in the autumn.

You'd really enjoy looking down on this view from the hills above; it's more like a superb painted picture than real countryside – wherever your eyes turn, they see nothing but a varied, harmonious and refreshing beauty.[15]

Another of his houses was on the coast near Ostia. It was near enough to Rome to get into town for business, but far enough away to offer real peace and quiet:

You sound surprised that I like my Laurentine (or as you put it, Laurentian) villa so much. You'll understand why, if I tell you how delightful the house is itself, how well it is situated, how wide a view it has of the sea. It is 17 kilometres from Rome; that means that once you've finished your day's work in town you can leave Rome and spend the night there. There are several ways to get to it, the roads to Laurentum and Ostia both lead there. You turn off the Laurentum road after 14 kilometres, the Ostia road after 11. The secondary road from both points is quite sandy, which makes the going slow and heavy for carriages, but light and easy for riding. The view on either side is varied: first the road narrows as it passes through a wood, then it widens as it passes rolling fields. Flocks of sheep, herds of cattle and horses, driven down from the hills by winter's cold, graze and grow fat on the grass there in the spring-like air.

In the same letter Pliny describes this house in great detail – enough for a plan and a model to have been made of it. You can see pictures on these pages. The next two quotations describe the main entrance of the house, and Pliny's own private apartments. They are marked on the plan on page 57.

My villa is just right for my needs, and not expensive to run. First you come into an *atrium*, moderately-sized but not mean; from it you go into a small but pleasant courtyard, enclosed by pillared walkways in the shape of a letter D. This is a good place to go in bad weather, because it is protected by glass windows and an overhanging roof. At its centre-point there is a door leading into a pleasant inner hall, and a rather nice dining-room which runs out along the beach. When the south wind stirs up the sea, the breakers along the shore wash it gently with flung spray. All round the dining-room are folding doors, or windows the size of doors, so that it appears to look out on three different seas at the front and sides; the back looks out on the inner hall, the courtyard and through the porticos the *atrium*; from there you can see the woods and the hills in the distance . . .

At the head of the terrace, covered way and garden is a separate building, my own favourite. I like it especially, because I had it built myself. In it

56

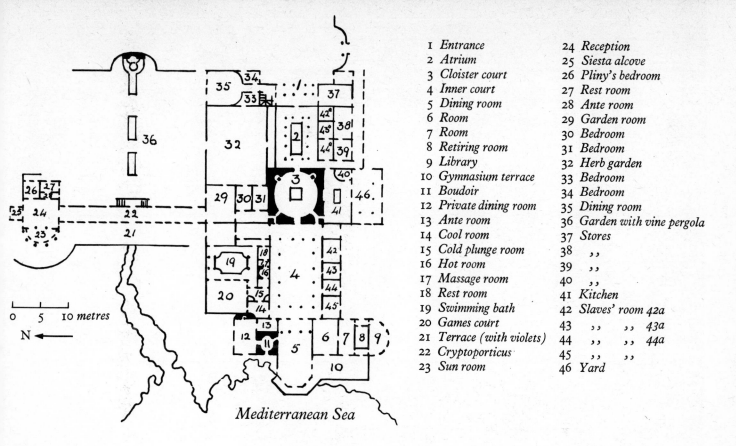

1	Entrance	24	Reception
2	Atrium	25	Siesta alcove
3	Cloister court	26	Pliny's bedroom
4	Inner court	27	Rest room
5	Dining room	28	Ante room
6	Room	29	Garden room
7	Room	30	Bedroom
8	Retiring room	31	Bedroom
9	Library	32	Herb garden
10	Gymnasium terrace	33	Bedroom
11	Boudoir	34	Bedroom
12	Private dining room	35	Dining room
13	Ante room	36	Garden with vine pergola
14	Cool room	37	Stores
15	Cold plunge room	38	,,
16	Hot room	39	,,
17	Massage room	40	,,
18	Rest room	41	Kitchen
19	Swimming bath	42	Slaves' room 42a
20	Games court	43	,, ,, 43a
21	Terrace (with violets)	44	,, ,, 44a
22	Cryptoporticus	45	,, ,,
23	Sun room	46	Yard

Mediterranean Sea

Pliny's villa. Above: *The ground plan.*

Left: *A reconstruction model, showing first the front portico and second the dining-room at the end of the right wing.*

there is a sun-room, looking out on one side to the terrace, on the other to the sea, and facing the sun on both sides. There is a room there with double doors on to the covered way, and a window overlooking the sea. Opposite the centre of the wall is a well-designed alcove, which can be added to the room (by folding back its windows and drawing the curtains) or shut off from it (by closing them). This alcove is large enough to hold a couch and two armchairs; it has the sea at its foot, other houses at its back, and woods at its head. These views can either be seen separately, each through its own window, or all at once.

Next to these rooms is a bedroom for sleeping in at night. Unless its windows are open, it is proof against the voices of slaves, the boom of the sea, the noise of storms, the flash of lightning – even daylight itself. The reason for this deep, secret quiet is that a passage runs down between the wall of the room and the garden, so that all noises are absorbed in empty

Hadrian's villa at Tivoli. The architect has taken the reflections into account when planning the building.

air. Beside the bedroom is a very small boiler-room, with a narrow outlet to let the stored heat in or out, whichever is required. Then there is a dressing-room and another bedroom, built to face the sun and catch its rays from sunrise right up into the afternoon, when they come in at a slant.

Whenever I withdraw to this building, I feel completely cut off from my villa. This is particularly useful at the Saturnalia, when every other part of the house is full of the noise and excitement of my slaves. I can shut myself off, so that they don't interrupt my work, and I don't interrupt their holiday.[16]

Certainly no civilised people before the Romans understood and loved the countryside as they did. Some of them, it's true, took a rather wistful, uncritical view of country folk:

Favourite Roman scenery includes water and poplar trees. This is the Spring of Clitumnus, a well-known beauty spot.

Their lives are peaceful, honest and secure;
They work hard, and when work is done they rest
In their own broad acres. Caves, rivers and lakes,
Cool valleys, cattle lowing, sleep in the shade
Of tall green trees, broad thickets full of game –
All this is theirs. As children they learned
Respect for the gods, respect for their parents.
It was here that Justice, leaving the earth for good,
Lingered a little. Her footprints still are here.[17]

Others, like Cato (whose book on farming is quoted on page 84) had a more practical attitude:

When someone asked him what was the best way of making money out of the land he replied, 'Raising cattle successfully.'
'And after that?'
'Raising cattle fairly successfully.'
'And after that?'
'Raising cattle unsuccessfully.'
'And after that?'

The courtyard of a wealthy man's villa, on the coast near Ostia.

'Raising crops.'
'How about moneylending?' the questioner then asked.
Cato replied, 'How about murder?'[18]

The final extract, a description of a farmer and his country festival, sums up a lot of what the Romans felt about the land. It fed them, kept them busy and happy, and provided the means of relaxation. The photos here show various parts of the Italian countryside – much of it just as it was when this poem was written.

Aquinum : remains of a Roman arch.

Come, join our festival: in an ancient rite
We are asking the gods to bless our fields and crops.
Horned Bacchus, lord of the vine, come down to us;
Ceres, queen of the golden harvest, come!
Today is a holiday: the fields must rest,
The farmers rest, the ploughshares work no more.
Unyoke the oxen; garland their heads, and fill
Their mangers full. No spinning; praise the gods!
If you made love last night, then you must stand
Aside: for Venus is not invited here today.
The gods love purity: wear clean clothes, wash
Your hands, and draw fresh water from the stream.
Look there: the altar-fire is burning; priests,
White-robed and garlanded with olive-leaves,
Are bringing a pure white lamb for sacrifice.

Hercules resting by a country shrine with his cattle.

Gods of our native land, now may all fields
And farmers by this act be purified;
Drive out evil forces from our lands;
Let no foul weeds destroy the rising corn,
No lamb be slaughtered by plundering wolves.
Then let the farmer (fat, with well-filled barns)
Pile logs on his hearth-fire, while children play –
Slave-children too, proof of a happy home –
Building straw-houses in the dust. Ah, look:
The sacrifice is clean, without a fault –
The gods have heard our prayer, and answered it.
Up from the cellar bring tall dusty jars
Of old Falernian and Chian wine,
Laid down in days beyond our memory.
Let wine complete our holiday – no shame
In getting tipsy at a festival.[19]

4 · At war

TIME: early in the fourth century B.C.
PLACE: Veii, a wealthy town in Etruria, about 24 kilometres north of Rome.

So the Roman army marched to Veii. Camillus tightened the ring of fortifications round the city and gave orders that no one was to start fighting unless ordered to. This put a stop to the number of rash and futile skirmishes that had been taking place between the wall and the Roman fortifications, and reserved the soldiers for the real jobs in hand. Of these, much the largest and toughest was the digging of a tunnel up into the central fortress of Veii. To keep the work going and to stop the men exhausting themselves by continuous underground labour, Camillus split up the workers into six shifts, to work six hours each in turn. The operation was planned to continue without pause until the fortress was reached.

Camillus saw that at last victory was his for the taking. He left his headquarters, ordered the troops to stand ready and prayed, 'Apollo, I am led and inspired by thee to destroy the city of Veii, and to thee I promise a tenth of the plunder. Thee also, Queen Juno, I pray to leave Veii and find thyself a new home, following us in our victorious return. In Rome shalt thou find a temple worthy of thy greatness.' The army moved forwards in overwhelming numbers from all directions, to distract attention from the imminent danger hidden in the tunnel.

The people of Veii did not know that their own prophets and foreign oracles had already foreseen their doom; they did not know that the gods had been promised a share in the plunder and, in answer to prayer, were looking now towards new homes in the temples of their enemies; they did not know that this was to be their last day. They had no suspicion of the tunnel or of the enemy troops who would soon come bursting into their

Etruscan warriors carrying a wounded comrade. The figures form the handle on the lid of a chest.

fortress. Every man armed himself and ran to the walls, wondering what was going on; for days now, the Romans had not moved from their posts and here they were running towards the walls as though they had suddenly gone mad.

The tunnel was now full of picked men. Suddenly they came bursting out, into the temple of Juno in the middle of the fortress. The men of Veii, looking outwards from the walls, were attacked from behind, bolts were wrenched off the gates and some of the Romans, under a hail of stones and tiles from the women and slaves on the rooftops, started to set fire to the houses. The air was thick with screams and shouts and the wailing of women and children. In a moment, men were being thrown off the walls and the gates were open. The rest of the Roman army poured in or climbed the undefended walls. The city was full of Romans and fighting raged everywhere. The men of Veii put up a tremendous resistance, but at last it began to slacken and Camillus ordered that all those not carrying weapons should be spared. That was the end of bloodshed. The unarmed men began to surrender and the Roman soldiers, with Camillus' permission, scattered to sack the town.[1]

This was one of the first serious campaigns the Romans faced. In this description we can see not only the bravery, on both sides, but on the Roman side organisation – in the timing of the simultaneous assaults (without watches!) and in the actual digging of the tunnel. The soldiers were armed according to a detailed schedule prepared over 100 years before by one of their kings, Servius Tullius:

Servius formed 80 centuries (groups of 100 men) from those who were worth 100,000 asses or more, 40 of older and 40 of younger men. Together, these two groups were known as the First Class. The older men were to guard Rome, the younger ones to go on active service. They all had to equip themselves with a helmet, round shield, leg-guards and breastplate, all of bronze. Apart from this armour, they had as their weapons a sword and a spear. Attached to this class were 2 centuries of unarmed engineers, whose job was to look after the siege-engines in the field.

The Second Class was drawn from men worth between 100,000 and 75,000. They formed 20 centuries, senior and junior, and were to be equipped like the First Class, except that they had no breastplate and a long shield instead of a round one.

The Third Class was of men worth 50,000. They were organised exactly like the Second Class, but they didn't have leg-guards.

The Fourth Class was of men worth 25,000. There were again 20 centuries of them, but their only equipment was a spear and a javelin.

The Fifth Class, of men worth 11,000, consisted of 30 centuries, armed with slings and stones. Also into this class came 2 centuries of buglers and trumpeters.

All those worth less than 11,000 were organised into 1 century, but were not called up.[2]

No doubt, in battle, the 30 centuries of slingers stood a good chance of being reduced to a more orthodox 20. The formation was still that of the Greek phalanx (see *Through Greek Eyes*, p. 9), but this proved unwieldy against lightly armed 'barbarians' so, about fifty years after the capture of Veii, the pattern was changed:

Previously, the Romans had used the small round shield, but after the introduction of pay for those serving in the army they changed over to the oblong one and what before had been a phalanx on the Macedonian

Reconstructed legionary armour.

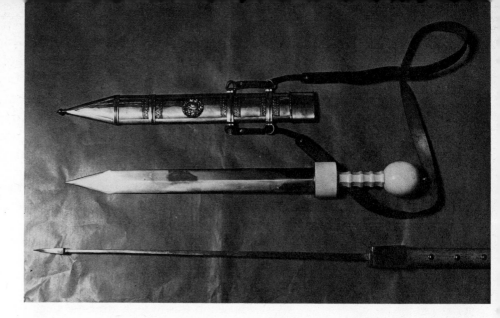

Reconstructed javelin, sword and sheath.

pattern now became a battle-line made up of maniples (groups of about 150). The troops to the rear were arranged in several companies.

The first line, the *hastati* (spearmen), was made up of 15 maniples with small gaps between them. In each maniple were 20 light-armed troops, the rest carrying oblong shields – the so-called 'light-armed' soldiers carried only javelins and a spear. This front line contained the flower of youth, fast approaching their military maturity. Behind them came a line of the same size, consisting of more experienced troops called *principes* (chiefs); they all carried oblong shields and wore the most splendid armour of anyone. This total force of 30 maniples was called the *antepilani* (vanguard) because behind the standards were another 15 companies, each split into 3 sections, the first of which was called *pilus*. A company consisted of 3 *vexilla* (literally, banners) and in each *vexillum* there were 60 soldiers, 2 centurions and 1 colour-bearer, making 189 men in each company. The first *vexillum* preceded the *triarii*, veterans who had proved themselves in battle; the second preceded the *rorarii*, who were younger and less experienced; the third the *accensi*, who were the least reliable and so placed in the rear.

When the army had been set out in this way, the *hastati* were the first to go into battle. If they were unable to beat the enemy, they retreated slowly and fell back into the gaps between the companies of the *principes*. The fighting was then taken up by the *principes* with the *hastati* in support. The *triarii* knelt under their standards with the left leg forward, their shields supported on their shoulders, their spears stuck in the ground and angled

Roman soldiers manoeuvring siege engines.

up at 45°, producing the effect of a palisade bristling with stakes. If the *principes* also got into difficulties, they retreated gradually to the *triarii* (that's where the old saying, 'We're back to the *triarii*' comes from, when things are going badly). The *triarii* would let the first two lines come back through the gaps between their companies and immediately close ranks; after which, with no further troops to fall back on, they would charge the enemy in one compact body. This was quite terrifying for the enemy who were, as they thought, delivering the fatal blow, when they suddenly saw this new, and larger, line of men rising up in front of them.

The army was usually of 4 legions, each 5,000 strong, with 300 cavalry to each legion.[3]

This reorganisation lasted for well over 200 years, until the reforms of Marius. But what of the individual soldier? He started off with an introduction to some ranking officer:

I was rather pressing in my request for you to make a friend of mine a military tribune, but you will realise why when you find out who he is and what sort of man. Now that you have promised to do this, I can give you his name and tell you about him. His name is Cornelius Minicianus and as far as nobility and character go he is the pride of our district. He comes from a good family, is well off, but is as fond of literature as any poor intellectual. He is also extremely honest in his legal judgements, a bold speaker and the most loyal of friends. When you get to know him better, you will find him good enough to tackle any job, to deserve any distinction, and you will then realise that I have done you a favour. As he is an extremely modest man, I will not say more.[4]

Here, Pliny the Younger uses the aristocratic network to help a young friend. But the practice seems to have been common among lower ranks as well. A soldier in Alexandria writes home to his father:

God willing, I hope I can manage without spending too much and get myself transferred to a cohort. But you can't get anywhere round here without money, and it's no use having testimonials if you don't help yourself.[5]

After some sort of introduction like this you were then put through the *probatio*, a combination of a medical examination and an interview. One of the jobs of the interviewer was to check your height:

I know that the army has always required a minimum height for recruits: only men of 1·88 metres, or 1·78 at the least, used to be accepted for the cavalry or for the leading cohorts of legions. But then in those days the number of applicants was higher, before the civil service began draining off the best of the young men. So, if pressed, go more by the applicant's strength than by his sheer size.[6]

These words, written by the military historian Vegetius at the end of the fourth century A.D., show that all was not well on the recruiting front. More evidence comes from two instructions, issued for a particular military levy by the joint emperors Valentinian and Valens and addressed to Magnus, vicar of Rome, and both dated 27 April A.D. 367:

In the thick of battle. Not surprisingly, the Romans appear to be winning.

a. The levy shall be made of men 1·7 metres high by common measure.
b. By decree of the emperor Constantine of blessed memory, Your Sincerity must not allow those who try and avoid active service by amputating their fingers to succeed in their design, if the victims of these self-inflicted wounds can still be useful to the state in some way or other.[7]

But if you volunteered for the regular army, and passed the *probatio*, you were then posted to a camp and training began:

The first thing recruits should learn is the military step. The most important thing in marching or fighting is for all soldiers to keep their ranks, and they can only do this if they have learnt to march quickly and evenly. An army that is split up and in no sort of order is always in great danger from the enemy. So, with the military step they should cover, in summer, 30 kilometres in 5 hours; if they are using the full step, which is quicker, then they should cover 35 kilometres in the same period.

They should also do some running, for an undefined time and distance. This is a particularly important part of a recruit's training: for attacking the enemy with greater energy, for occupying strategic positions quickly when he has to or for getting there before the enemy can, for scouting at speed, for retreating quickly, or for catching up with an enemy in retreat. They must practise jumping, crossing ditches or tall obstacles, so that they can deal with the same situations when they meet them in the field. In the

69

Trajan's army crosses the Danube.

summer months all recruits ought to learn how to swim. Not all rivers have bridges over them, and as a soldier you often have to swim in retreat and in attack. Recruits must regularly be made to carry anything up to 35 kilos while marching with the military step.[8]

After this, you were trained in battle formations: single line, double

Lake Trasimene as it is now. Since Hannibal's time the shore-line has receded.

line, square, wedge, circle etc. Only at the end of this training were you allowed to fight for Rome; and not every battle turned out so well as the attack on Veii:

Flaminius gave the order to advance and to lift the standards out of the ground. He then jumped into the saddle, but as he did so the horse suddenly stumbled and threw the consul head first to the ground. All those standing near were terrified enough by this unlucky sign, but that was not all: a message came that the standard-bearer had tried with all his strength to lift the standard, but it was stuck fast. Flaminius turned to the soldier who had brought the message. 'Don't tell me you've got a letter from the Senate too, saying I mustn't fight? Go and tell them, if they're too weak with fright to pull the standard up, then they can dig it up!' The army began to move forward . . .

They reached Lake Trasimene at sunset. No reconnaissance was made, but the next morning, almost before it was light, they entered the narrow pass. As they reached the wider part of the plain the army began to spread

Hannibal.

Scipio Africanus – hardly flattering, but for that reason possibly a good likeness.

out. Flaminius now saw the enemy troops who were straight ahead of him, but had no idea of those behind and those in the hills above him. Hannibal's trap had worked: Flaminius was surrounded by the lake, the hills and the Carthaginians. Hannibal gave the order, to attack from three directions at once. Down they came, on whatever Roman troops lay in their path. The Romans were in a panic, made worse by the early-morning mist which had risen off the lake and now lay in the flat ground between the hills; whereas the Carthaginians, being on the high ground, could still see each other and coordinate their attack. Even before the Romans could see what had happened, the shouting all around told them that they were trapped . . .

Wherever they tried to turn, their way was blocked; to left and right, hills and the lake; to front and rear, the enemy army. It was clear now that hope lay only in fighting their way out and every man became his own commander. The battle took a new turn. The regular battle formations, ranks, legions, cohorts, all were abandoned. Chance was the only organising factor, and a soldier's position in the battle was a measure of his will to fight. It was a ferocious struggle leaving time for no other thoughts. There was an earthquake at the same time, which wrecked whole areas of several large cities in Italy, brought floods sweeping down from rivers and the sea and triggered off avalanches in the mountains; no one on the battlefield noticed it.[9]

The more religious among the survivors blamed Flaminius for ignoring the unlucky signs that the gods sent him. Anyone might reasonably blame him for not making a reconnaissance. Livy puts the Roman casualties in this and the next battle, near Cannae, at a total of 65,000 men. Incredibly, the Romans held out in this war: fifteen years later, under the command of Scipio, some of the survivors of Lake Trasimene may well have been fighting Hannibal in the final battle at Zama, on the northern fringe of the Sahara desert:

Scipio did not organise his troops with each cohort in front of its standard as usual, but in small groups, leaving lanes between them through which the elephants could charge without doing any damage. Scipio blocked the entrances to these lanes with light-armed auxiliary troops. They had been told that, when the elephants charged, they were either to retreat to the rear or to swing left and right to bring them immediately behind the front-

An elephant displaying its usefulness in close fighting.

line troops; either way, the elephants would pass through between two fires. Hannibal had put his elephants right in the front of his army, to try and crack the Roman morale – he had eighty of them, more than he had ever used in battle before . . .

He was still addressing his Carthaginian troops, when the Roman bugles and trumpets sounded, and such a terrific shout went up that the elephants, particularly on the left flanks, turned against their own side. The confusion was increased by Masinissa on the Roman right flank, who drove the African cavalry away from the main army. But there were a few elephants who had not panicked and they charged the Romans. Although badly wounded in the process, they began to cause terrible destruction in the ranks of the auxiliaries, who leapt for cover to each side and then caught the animals in cross-fire with their spears. Meanwhile the front rank kept up an attack with their javelins, until the elephants, under attack from every quarter, swung away from the Roman army and charged their own right wing. Even Carthaginian cavalry could not face that, and they fled. So, stripped of all cavalry support, their infantry closed with that of the

Gnaeus Domitius Corbulo.

Romans, but they were not now fairly matched either in morale or stamina . . .

The Roman cavalry commanders, Laelius and Masinissa, had chased the enemy cavalry for some little distance and now returned at just the right moment to charge the rear of their infantry. This cavalry charge clinched the battle. Numbers of the Carthaginians were surrounded and slaughtered where they stood; many tried to escape, but on that wide plain there was no protection from the death-dealing cavalry. That day, Carthage and her allies lost more than 20,000 men, and about the same number were taken prisoner, with 132 military standards and eleven elephants. Roman casualties were about 1,500.[10]

Nothing is said of the extreme heat in which the battle was fought. Roman soldiers were expected to cope with all weathers and temperatures, but they did not always live up to these expectations:

Corbulo had more trouble dealing with his own soldiers' slackness than with the enemy's treachery. His legions had come to Asia Minor from Syria, where they had enjoyed years of peace and grown slack, and so they were extremely reluctant to undergo the rigours of service in the field. We know that in that army there were veterans who had never been on guard or on watch and who regarded ramparts and ditches as novel curiosities. They didn't possess helmets or breastplates; they were just fleshy profiteers who had spent their whole army life in towns.

So Corbulo discharged the ones who were too old or too ill to be any good, and to fill their places held a recruiting drive in Galatia and Cappadocia. His numbers were also strengthened by a legion from Germany together with their auxiliary infantry and cavalry. The whole army was kept under canvas in spite of the savage cold; the ground was so encrusted with ice that the soldiers had to excavate foundations for the tents. Numbers of soldiers lost arms or legs because of frostbite and some sentries were frozen to death. There is the story, too, of one soldier carrying a bundle of firewood; his hands were so frozen that they fell off, still clutching their load.[11]

Between the time of Zama and of Corbulo's campaign, the self-made, tough military genius, Caius Marius, put the final touch to reforms already in progress. The aristocratic commanders, like Flaminius at

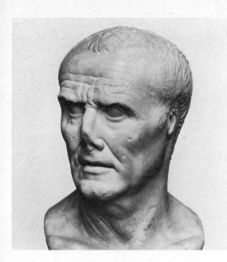

Possibly Marius: certainly someone whose wishes should not be lightly thwarted.

Trasimene, had been having no success against the enemy, an African prince called Jugurtha. From the story told by the historian Sallust we get an idea of Marius' approach to life:

Compare me, gentlemen, the 'new' man, with these lordly ones. What they have heard of, or read, I have either seen or done with my own hands; what they have learnt from books, I have learnt from experience. Words or deeds: which are more to the point, do you think? They despise my humble origin, I despise their idleness. But if my origin is thrown in my face, I can accuse them of criminal actions . . . Perhaps they're right to despise me.

In that case, they might despise their own ancestors who won their nobility like me, by their merits. They envy my rise to power. They ought to envy the sheer hard work, then, and the dangers which I have put up with to get to the top . . . When they address you, or the Senate, they spend most of their time praising their ancestors. They obviously think that by reminding you of these men's bravery they are adding brightness to their own image. Far from it! The finer the lives of their ancestors, the more shameful their own feebleness . . . I cannot fill you with confidence in my ability by pointing to portraits, triumphs or consulships of my ancestors. What I can show you, if I have to, are spears, a banner, medals and other honours of war, not to mention the scars on my body, and all of them in front. Here are my family portraits, my proofs of nobility. They were not handed down to me, either, like the virtues of these men. I won them myself by long, hard, dangerous fighting.[12]

Marius succeeded where the aristocrats failed, not only by hard work, but because his approach was completely professional. One of the most important points in his reform was to abolish conscription: farmers no longer had to fear that they would be hauled off to Africa just as the harvest was ready. He also increased the soldiers' pay. Here is an example of his professional and open-minded attitude:

The drill for weapon-training was introduced to the soldiers by the consul P. Rutilius, colleague of Cn. Mallius. Going against tradition, he summoned the trainers of the gladiators from the school of C. Aurelius Scaurus and created in the legions a more sophisticated technique of avoiding and delivering blows. He united courage with craft and craft with

Ancestral portraits on a tomb: Caius Rabirius, his wife and Usia, high priestess of Isis.

courage: craft was made bolder by the vehemence of courage, courage more circumspect by the awareness of craft.[13]

Caius Marius had the opportunity of selecting his army out of two that were in existence, one that had served under Rutilius and one under Metellus, which Marius himself had later commanded. He chose Rutilius', even though it was smaller, because he thought it was the better trained of the two.[14]

Coin of Vercingetorix.

Right: *Remains of Alesia, Vercingetorix's capital.*

This new, professional, Roman army reached a high point of efficiency fifty years later under Marius' nephew, Julius Caesar. In the next example, Caesar is besieging Alesia, the stronghold in Central Gaul of the Gallic chieftain Vercingetorix, and it may be interesting to compare his methods with those of Camillus 350 years before:

Caesar dug a trench 6 metres wide with perpendicular sides, so that it was the same breadth at the top and bottom, and put the rest of the siege

77

Julius Caesar. A different face from the coin on page 19 – but very like the statue on page 79.

equipment 350 metres behind it. He had to enclose a very large area which couldn't easily be protected by a circle of troops, so his idea was to guard against any sudden attack the enemy might make against troops building the siege-works. At this distance of 350 metres he dug two more trenches round the hill, 4 metres wide and the same depth, and filled the inner one – which was on low, flat ground – with water diverted from the river. Behind these trenches he built a ramp 3 metres high, complete with palisade. He added a parapet and battlements and a row of horizontal stakes at the point where the ramp and parapet joined, to make it harder for the enemy to climb up. Round the whole thing he put up towers at 20-metre intervals.[15]

Caesar was not only efficient: he also had what we would call an 'image'. As the soldiers sang at one of his triumphal processions through the streets of Rome:

Lock up your wives! Old Baldy's back
And dying to pay a 'social' call.
Your cash? You won't see that again:
He used it up on girls in Gaul.[16]

More flattering, perhaps, is a portrait of him from 100 years after his death:

Caesar possessed not merely a name and reputation as a soldier, but some inner force that pushed him ever onwards. The only thing he shrank from was defeat. Fierce, untameable in pursuit of his expectations, he battled on, sparing no bloodshed. Success acted only as a spur; riding his luck, sweeping all obstacles aside, he headed for the heights and rejoiced in his devastating progress.[17]

But, as Corbulo found to his cost, it was possible for a Roman soldier never to throw his spear in anger. His enemy then was boredom. There was nothing left but wine, women, draughts and beating up the local population, with one excuse or another. Germanicus, the adopted son of the emperor Tiberius, writes to Alexandria in A.D. 19:

I am informed that boats and animals are being requisitioned with a view to my forthcoming visit, that lodgings are being forcibly occupied and

Caesar in his general's uniform. Both pictures demonstrate something of his powerful character and of his weak sense of humour.

private persons browbeaten. I think it necessary to point out that I do not want boats or beasts of burden to be seized by anyone, nor lodgings to be occupied, unless orders have been given by Baebius, my friend and secretary. If need be, Baebius himself will allot lodgings fairly and justly, and for boats and animals which we requisition I insist that fees are paid according to the list I have made. Anyone who disobeys these instructions should be brought before my secretary: he will either see that no individual suffers, or else report the matter to me. And nobody is to take by force any beasts of burden he comes across in the streets of the city. This is robbery, pure and simple.[18]

Sometimes the soldiers must have done civilian jobs – Pliny writes to Trajan:

I should like your advice, sir, on a point that is worrying me: should I go on using public slaves to guard the prisons, as has been done so far in the towns of my province, or should I use soldiers? I'm afraid that the public slaves are rather unreliable, but on the other hand I realise that this job would need quite a large number of soldiers. For the time being I have put a few soldiers on duty with the slaves, but I can quite see the danger, that neither party will do the job properly when each can blame the other for anything that goes wrong.

Trajan replies:

My dear Pliny, there is no need for more soldiers to be used as prison warders. We should keep to the traditional method of your province and use public slaves – their efficiency depends on your keenness and discipline. As you say, the danger in mixing soldiers with public slaves is that each will leave everything to the other party. And we should not be sticking to the general rule, of taking as few soldiers as possible away from their real job.[19]

'As few as possible' indicates that sometimes it had to be done. We may, finally, ask what the ordinary Roman in Rome thought of the wars, fought, it was claimed, on his behalf. Some Romans certainly disapproved:

The Romans are the only men on earth who attack poor and rich with the

A wounded Gaul – begging for mercy or shouting defiance?

Cleopatra – more intelligent than beautiful?

same enthusiasm. Robbery, murder, rape, are all disguised under the name 'empire'. They make a desert and call it 'peace'.[20]

This opinion was put by Tacitus into the mouth of a British chieftain, a wise precaution under the rule of an emperor. The only type of war that could, in retrospect anyway, be openly condemned, was civil war. Rome was torn with it for fifty years, on and off, between 80 and 30 B.C., when Sulla, Caesar, Pompey, Antony and Augustus were all struggling for power. The poet Horace writes about the final stages of the war around 35 B.C., between Antony and Cleopatra on one side and Augustus on the other:

Where are you rushing, madmen, where? And why
Do your right hands hold fast to hidden swords?
Why do you long to spill more Roman blood
On land and sea? I do not speak of wars
To burn the towers of hated Carthage or

Above: *Pompey the Great in middle age. By this time his glory had begun to fade, together with his good looks.*

Right: *Mark Antony, Caesar's right-hand man and later Cleopatra's lover.*

Far right: *The young Octavian (Augustus). Like Alexander, he inherited a civilisation in his teens.*

To lead the untamed Briton to his death
In chains. I speak of wars in which the prayers
Of our most bitter enemies are answered, wars
In which Rome turns her arms against herself.
What wolf or lion, for all its savagery
To other beasts, has ever acted thus?
Has some blind fury seized you? Are you rack'd
With stronger passions, then, with shame or guilt?
Answer me! They are silent. Faces pale,
They stand, their brains struck senseless. It is true;
The Romans flee before the lash of fate.
A brother's murder! Peace is now no more
Since Remus' death, bloody and undeserved,
Called forth a curse on his posterity.[21]

Few people can be enthusiastic about civil war, in any age. But is it possible to justify war at all? Cicero gives the politician's view:

There are two ways of settling a quarrel: by discussion and by force. Discussion is the proper human way, force is the way of wild animals, so we must use force only as a last resort, when discussion is impossible. It follows, therefore, that the only reason for us to start a war is so that we can live safely and in peace.[22]

But for a rank and file soldier, coming from northern Greece to fight and die in Britain, the philosophy of war was probably of little interest or importance – less important, no doubt, than just doing his duty.

The tomb of Rufus Sita, a Thracian cavalryman, who died at Gloucester aged forty after twenty-two years' service.

5 · Ordinary people

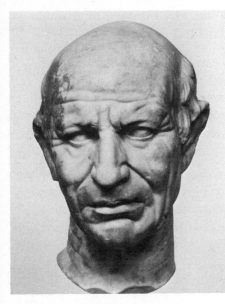

Head of an elderly man, possibly a slave.

When Augustus was emperor of Rome (27 B.C.–A.D. 14), there were probably about 500,000 free men and women living in the city, and about 280,000 slaves. These inhabitants were grouped into three citizen classes and one non-citizen group:

1. *The Senate:* 600 of the leading noblemen, chosen from those who held high political office.

2. *The Knights:* no one knows how many there were. (The number usually given varies between 5,000 and 10,000.) Any free man could become a Knight as long as he was a Roman citizen and owned capital worth at least 400,000 sesterces.* Some of the Knights were multi-millionaires (in sesterces), and many leading bankers and civil servants came from this class.

3. *The Plebeians:* ordinary people – soldiers, craftsmen, shopkeepers and the owners of small businesses.

4. *Non-citizens:* all slaves, and freedmen awaiting citizenship.

Unfortunately for us, only the two upper groups were really concerned with literature: in fact the majority of Roman citizens may never have learned to read or write at all. This means that most of the Roman literature we possess today consists of upper-class writings on life and culture. The greatest authors – Cicero, Pliny and Virgil, for example – were quite rich men, whose day-to-day life was very different from that of ordinary citizens. The general attitude of such men to those less nobly-born comes clearly across from the following letter on slaves, written by one rich nobleman to another.

* No real value can be given for the sestertius in modern money. You could buy a meal with plenty of wine for 1 sestertius; an average-sized house would cost something like 20,000 sesterces.

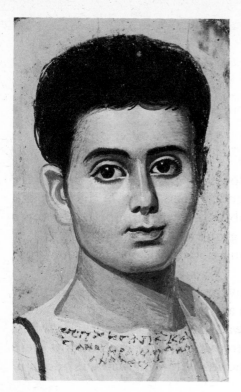

Egyptian portrait of the second century A.D. *showing a rich young man, probably Roman or half-Roman by birth.*

Your recent visitors have told me how friendly you are with your slaves. This pleases me: it shows that you live up to your principles, and put your philosophical training into practice. 'They're only slaves', people will object. Maybe, but they're human beings like ourselves. 'But they're *slaves!*' They live in the same house as us. 'But they're still slaves!' I'd rather call them friends – humble friends. For after all, if they *are* slaves, so are we – for Fate rules us just as much as them.[1]

Even if you regarded your slaves with as much fellow-feeling as that, they were still a business commodity like any other. They had to be used carefully, sparingly and totally without sentiment:

Food for the slaves. (1) Labourers should get 4 measures* of grain in the winter months, and $4\frac{1}{2}$ measures in summer. (2) The chief hand, the housekeeper, the foreman and the head shepherd should get 3 measures each. (3) The chain-gang: in winter each man should get $1\frac{1}{2}$ kilos of bread daily; from vine-digging till fig-ripening time 2 kilos daily, then back to $1\frac{1}{2}$ again.

Wine for the slaves. For the first 3 months after the grape-harvest, they should drink wine made from the skin and pips; in the 4th month they should get $\frac{1}{3}$ litre daily, or 10 litres altogether. In the 5th–8th months this ration should be doubled, and in the 9th–12th months they should get 1 litre daily, or 30 litres per month per man. At the December festivals of *Saturnalia* and *Compitalia* each man should get an extra 15 litres. The total wine given to each man in a year should be about 250 litres. The chain-gang should get extra, depending what work they're doing. Their annual amount should be about 320 litres per man.

Pickles and sauce for the slaves. Keep as many windfall olives as possible, and all the ripe ones that will only give a little oil. Issue them sparingly: make them last as long as possible. When they're finished, give the slaves pickled fish and sour wine. Each man should get $\frac{1}{2}$ litre olive oil per month, and 1 measure of salt should last him a whole year.

Clothes for the slaves. A tunic $1\frac{1}{4}$ metres long, and a cloak, every two years –

---

* It isn't clear how much this was, or how often it was given, or how many people it was meant to feed. A 'measure' was equal to an old English 'peck' – about enough to fill an average-sized bucket. If this is so, then 4 measures would feed one man for a month, or one man and his dependants for a week.

Estate work : milking goats.

and whenever you issue a new tunic or cloak, take back the old ones for patching. You should see that each slave gets a good pair of clogs every second year.[2]

The chain-gang mentioned here would consist of slaves who were particularly dangerous: ex-convicts or men with a bad record for trying to escape. They were kept chained up in long lines, and used for the heaviest jobs, like road-mending and ditch-digging. These were the heaviest jobs, but ordinary farmwork was heavy enough – simply because of the amount each slave was expected to get through.

Cato calculates the numbers of slaves needed for estate-work using two factors: the size of the farm and the type of crop. He gives, for example, different calculations for olive-estates and vineyards. His first calculation is for an olive-grove of 240 Roman acres. He says that an estate this size needs 13 slaves – 1 foreman, 1 housekeeper, 5 labourers, 3 cowherds, 1 muleteer, 1 swineherd, and 1 shepherd. The second calculation is for a vineyard of 100 Roman acres: this needs 15 slaves – 1 foreman, 1 housekeeper, 10 labourers, 1 cowherd, 1 muleteer and 1 swineherd. Saserna writes that you need 1 slave for every 8 acres, and that it should take him 45 days to dig them over – 4 days' digging per acre, plus 13 days for idleness, bad weather, illness or careless work.[3]

(A Roman acre was approximately 75 metres long by 35 metres wide: that is, just over half the size of an English acre.)

In the same passage the author tells us how to treat the slaves in order to get maximum use out of them. The sad thing about this passage is how clearly it shows some masters regarding their slaves as robots or pet animals, forgetting that (in the words of our first extract) 'they're human beings like ourselves'.

A sleeping slave boy.

You shouldn't let your farmhands' spirits get too low – or too high. Your foremen should be able to read and write: they should be quiet men of good character, and older than the labourers (who will obey older men more willingly than younger ones). The one essential qualification is that your foremen should know all there is to know about farming. They should not only give orders, but should take part in the work themselves, so that the labourers can imitate what they do, and realise that it's right for them to have authority because they have greater experience. Don't let your overseers use whips, if they can get the same results with encouragement.

Don't buy too many slaves of the same nationality: this always leads to domestic squabbling. Get your foremen to cooperate with you by giving them bonuses, and allowing them to mate for life with female slaves, and have children. This will make them more loyal, and attach them more firmly to the farm. It's this sort of relationship that makes slave-families from Epirus so sought-after and so expensive.

Give your overseers privileges, and they'll respect you for it. Consult the better-quality labourers, too, about the work to be done – this makes them feel less despised and more respected by their owner. You'll find your slaves work better if you treat them well, and give them extra food or clothing, days off, permission to graze their own cattle on your land, or other similar privileges. If you do this, you can win back the loyalty and goodwill even of men you've had to punish or drive hard for a long time.[4]

An old slave, possibly a fisherman.

Of course when slaves were treated like animals they behaved like animals. When Spartacus – an escaped gladiator – led the Slave Revolt in 73 B.C., his followers behaved with such ferocity, and were so numerous, that it took the Roman army two long years to defeat them. And minor atrocities like this one were always happening:

Larcius Macedo, a gentleman of high rank, was attacked not long ago by his own slaves. No letter can do justice to such an outrage. I grant you he was a proud and cruel master; he preferred to forget – or perhaps remembered only too well – that his own father had once been a slave. He was taking a bath in his villa near Formiae, when his slaves suddenly surrounded and attacked him. One went for his throat, another punched him in the face, and another beat him about the chest and ribs, and (worse still) the private parts.

At last they thought he was dead, and threw him down on the hot stones to make sure. He lay there motionless, either because he really was unconscious or because he wanted them to think so. They decided that he must be dead, carried him out (pretending that he'd collapsed from the heat) and handed him over to some more trustworthy slaves. His concubines ran up yelling and screaming; the noise and the cooler air revived him, and he stirred and opened his eyes – it was safe now to show that he was still alive.

The slaves fled; most of them were recaptured, and the rest are being hunted. Macedo himself lived only for a few days; but he died with the satisfaction of knowing that his death had been avenged and his murderers punished – something few victims live to enjoy.

These are the dangers, ill-treatment and insults we slave-owners risk – and it's no use hoping to escape by being kind or affectionate. After all, it's not reason that makes slaves murder their master, it's their own criminal natures.[5]

The comment about Macedo's father is very shrewd. But Macedo was no crueller a master than most. If a slave fell sick or grew old, for example, he was no more use to his owner than a worn-out curtain or a broken cooking-pot. 'Businesslike' masters sent some to the arena to feed the lions, or abandoned them to die; others were often executed on the spot. These practices were so widespread that the emperor Claudius passed a law to try and stop them:

Slaves hauling a barge full of barrels.

A number of slave-owners had abandoned sick or elderly slaves on the island of Aesculapius, to avoid having to pay for medical treatment. Claudius ordered all these slaves to be set free, and decreed that they were not to be returned to their owners if they recovered. He also decreed that anyone who killed a sick slave instead of curing him was to be arrested and charged with murder.[6]

Of course there were kind-hearted masters as well, men who treated their slaves generously, and were liked and respected by them. Pliny's comments, for example, show that he was a humane and generous man, whose slaves probably considered themselves very lucky to be in his service. On one occasion he writes to a friend:

I'm always very upset when my slaves fall ill and die, especially the younger ones. There are two consolations – not equal to the grief, but still consolations. The first is that I am able to set them free before they die – for it seems to me that freedom does slightly ease the pain of an early death. The second is that I allow even slaves to make a will, and I obey it as though it was a genuine legal document. They give instructions and make legacies as they see fit; I carry out their wishes as though under orders. They can make whatever gifts or bequests they choose, provided it's kept within the household – for I consider that the household is a slave's own country, so to speak: the one area where he has a kind of citizenship of his own.[7]

So the outlook for slaves wasn't entirely bleak. They might be given their freedom in the way described above, or after long and faithful service; they could also save up tips and presents (if any) until they had enough money to buy their own liberty. Some freedmen went on working afterwards for the same master, doing the same work but earning a small wage; others struck out on their own, and made a living by hiring themselves out in the market-place. Here is a discussion between a customer (Ballio) and a freedman cook, who knows exactly what his services are worth, and also how to blind his customers with science:

BALLIO Cook Square, they call it – Swindler Square would be more like it! Look at this so-called cook: if I'd promised to find a bigger cheat, I couldn't have managed it! Just look at him: big talk, big mouth, big head, big waste of time. The only reason he hasn't gone to Hell is that they need someone up here to cook for corpses – at any rate, only a corpse would enjoy the sort of food *he* cooks.

COOK If that's how you feel, why did you hire me?

BALLIO No choice – everyone else had gone. Anyway, if you *are* such a brilliant cook, why are you the only one left?

COOK That's not *my* brilliance, it's *their* meanness.

BALLIO Pardon?

COOK The customers', I mean. When people come here for a cook, it's not the best they want, it's the cheapest. That's why I'm the only one left. The others are a miserable lot: 1 drachma, and they're up and away. But *I* won't stir for less than 2. And then again, I don't cook like they do, piling the plates with cattle-fodder – *I* don't treat my guests like cows! Greens, greens, greens, that's all they know about. Even the flavouring's green: coriander, fennel, garlic, parsley, sorrel, cabbage, spinach, all buried under pounds of silphium and grated mustard so strong it grates on the slaves who grate it – look in the kitchen, you'll see them crying their eyes out. Cooks, *that* lot? It's not flavouring they put on their dishes, but owls that peck out the guests' guts and leave them 'owling for mercy. People die young round here – and no wonder,

Upstairs, downstairs.

the way they stuff themselves with greens whose *names* are dangerous, never mind their *taste*. Men in these parts eat plants no self-respecting cow would look at.

BALLIO And you're different, I suppose? Your flavouring's fit for the gods, keeps men alive instead of polishing them off?

COOK Exactly. Eat the food I cook, and you'll live 200 years. You wait till you taste my seasonings: a pinch of hotsitup, a spoonful of sweetansour, a pinch of pepransalt, and even the plates sit up and beg. Mind you, those seasonings are only for fish-dishes: for land-meat I always use bitothis, bitothat and takemin.

BALLIO You won't take *me* in! To Hell with you! What a load of rubbish![8]

Freedmen could reach the heights in the business and social world, but noblemen made it as difficult as possible. Cicero says here what was, and was not, the done thing:

On the question of the vulgarity or decency of trading and other ways of making a living, the general opinion seems to be as follows: the most despicable jobs are those which arouse people's hatred, like those of

A tax-collector, his slaves and his 'customers'.

customs officers and moneylenders. Any hired workman, also, who is paid for effort rather than skill is earning his living in an ungentlemanly and vulgar fashion. The money they get is really a badge of slavery.

Vulgarity is also attached to the retailers who buy direct from wholesalers and sell the product immediately, because they can only make a profit by a certain amount of lying, and there's nothing lower than such misleading behaviour. All factory workers are engaged in vulgar pursuits, because no factory can have anything spiritual about it. The most regrettable trades of all are those which deal in pleasures of the flesh: 'fishmongers, butchers, cooks, poulterers, fishermen', as the playwright Terence says. If you like, you can add to this list sellers of perfume, dancers, and the whole entertainment-crowd.

But those professions which demand a high level of intelligence or do a reasonable amount of good, like medicine, architecture and teaching, these are respectable if you belong to the proper class. Trade, though, is disreputable if on a small scale; on a large scale, if it involves large networks of transportation and distributes a variety of goods without false descriptions, it is not to be heavily condemned. And if the merchant has had his fill, or should I say has had enough, and retires metaphorically from the high seas of trade into port, or in actual fact from the port to a country estate, then he is highly respectable.

Of all the ways of making money, nothing is better than agriculture.[9]

Even if you married money, it didn't always help:

There was no better barber once in Rome
   Than you, dear Cinnamus, until your wife
      Bought you a passage to the bourgeoisie
And took you to a new, Sicilian home
   To lead a nobler, richer, better life.
      What will you do there? Will you be
A teacher in the art of speaking well,
   A schoolmaster for youths, or tots, or – no?
      A Cynic – no? You'll be a Stoic then?
Or when a theatre needs applause, you'll sell
   Your lusty voice? Well, what then? Ah, I know!
      You'll have to be a barber once again.[10]

Claudius, Emperor and God.

But some freedmen did succeed, and became both wealthy and powerful. The emperor Claudius was notorious for the powers he granted freedmen, allowing them to run practically the whole of his civil service. This enraged many of the noblemen, who felt that they'd been passed over in favour of men who not only had once been slaves, but were often foreigners into the bargain (mostly Greeks). The gossip-writer Suetonius echoes their disapproval:

Claudius' favourite freedman was the eunuch Posides. In the triumph celebrating Claudius' victory in Britain, he even went so far as to award Posides a medal just like the genuine soldiers. No less favoured was Felix: Claudius put him in command of infantry and cavalry squadrons and appointed him governor of Judaea. This man married three queens. There was also Harpocras, who was allowed to ride through Rome in a litter, and given the privilege of putting on gladiatorial shows. Even more highly regarded was Claudius' secretary Polybius, who often walked in processions between the consuls.

But the emperor's greatest favourites were his personal assistant Narcissus and his court treasurer Pallas. He willingly sanctioned a decree of the Senate which not only gave these men huge fortunes in money, but made them quaestors and praetors into the bargain. He allowed them such freedom in financial matters – and they got money by any means they could, fair or foul – that once, when he complained that the Royal Purse was almost empty, some wit not unreasonably said, 'He'd have a fortune, if only a couple of freedmen took him into partnership.'

The elaborate tombstone of a wealthy freedman, Amemptus, who had been the slave of Augustus' wife, Livia.

He was so influenced by freedmen and wives that he seemed more a servant than an emperor. On their instructions – that's to say, following their whims and wishes – he handed out offices of state, the command of armies, pardons and punishments. For most of the time he was quite unaware of this, and had no idea of the extent of their influence.[11]

Claudius ruled from A.D. 41 to 54. But even 250 years earlier, the same hostility to foreigners is evident, this time in a play written for a lower-class audience:

And as for those bloody Greeks, walking along with muffled-up heads, their cloaks bulging with books and shopping-baskets . . . They stand around gabbling at each other, the swine, blocking your way, bumping into you, and prancing along with their high-flown talk. You see them all the time, drinking in a pub when they've pinched something – heads wrapped up in their cloaks, full of hot drinks: there they go, half-tight and sad with it. If I come up against any of 'em, I'll give them a thump that'll bring up porridge with the wind.[12]

For aristocrats, much of what was said there would apply equally well to Romans of the lower class. Even their pleasures aroused well-bred scorn:

I've spent the last few days in peace and quiet, surrounded by my books and papers. 'What', you say, 'in *Rome*?' Yes: the Races were on – and they don't interest me at all. They never change, never vary: when you've seen one, you've seen them all. It really surprises me that so many thousands of grown men gather together as eagerly as children, to gape at galloping horses and people riding chariots. If it was the speed of the horses or skill of the drivers that attracted them, there would be some point in it – but it's only the colours worn by the drivers that they go to see. The colours are all that interest them; if the drivers changed colours during the race, the whole crowd would change with them, abandoning the horses and drivers they can identify from far off, and whose names they were so enthusiastically shouting a moment before.

That's the power a single worthless coloured shirt has over people – and not just ordinary people either, who are even simpler than the shirt. There are men of sense there too; and when I think how much time they

The emperor Theodosius and his courtiers, watching horse-racing.

waste, how enthusiastic they get over nothing, I take some pleasure in the fact that the Races give *me* no pleasure at all. So, I've spent this last holiday very comfortably working at my books, leaving it to everyone else to waste their time.[13]

The hint of snobbery in that letter is echoed in another writer's comments on gladiatorial shows:

I can think of nothing worse for the character than going to the Games. Even if you enjoy them, they offer an open door for vice to enter your character. At any rate, that's my experience: whenever I go to the Games I come back greedier, more ambitious and more extravagant – I'm crueller and less human simply because I've mixed with other human beings.

Racing to the turning-posts.

Not long ago I dropped in at the Midday Games, expecting an animal show, something amusing or relaxing that might distract men's eyes from the sight of human blood. But I was disappointed: there had been some fights earlier, but they were mild by comparison. Now we were being given a display of simple butchery. Men were fighting with no protective clothing of any kind. Their whole bodies were open to the blows, and no thrust ever missed its mark. Most of the audience prefer this to equally-matched contests, or request bouts. And it's hardly surprising: without helmets or shields to deflect the swords, there's no need of skill, and no chance of defence – and skill and defence would only put off the moment of killing. In the morning men are thrown to lions and bears; at midday they are thrown to their own spectators. Those who have killed fight those who will kill them, and the winners are then reserved for someone else to kill later on. The conclusion of every fight is death – by fire and sword. This is what goes on while the arena is empty.

'What of it?' you may ask. 'They're thieves after all – and murderers.' Ah! You mean that if you commit murder, you must be publicly butchered for it? And what crimes have *you* committed, to be forced to watch?

Gladiators in action.

'Kill!' they shout. 'Beat him! Burn him! Why won't he face the sword? What a coward! Why can't he die more eagerly? Beat his wounded back – they must strike each other's bare chests! Oh – it's the interval. Well, let's have someone strangled: we must have *something* to watch.'[14]

Reading that extract, it's hard to say which disgusts the writer more, the Games themselves, or the people watching them. But this attitude to the 'lower classes' is very common, throughout Roman history. Many aristocrats regarded ordinary people (the 'plebeians') as a vast, untrustworthy mob, to be feared or kept at a distance with bribes and festivals. The words of the satirist Juvenal must have appealed to many of his aristocratic readers. Seianus, the chief minister of the aged emperor Tiberius, had made a bid for power, failed, and been executed. As Seianus' corpse is dragged through the streets of Rome, Juvenal looks at the watching crowds and reflects:

And what do the common people think? No change: they follow Fate,

Children learning to handle horses. The tutor stands on the left.

and kick men when they're down. If old Tiberius had suddenly died, and Fate had favoured Seianus, *he'd* be emperor now. Their votes aren't worth selling any more: once they'd power, position and wealth to give away, but now they're tamed, they know their place – up on their hind legs, begging for just two things: Bread and Entertainment.[15]

Free food and endless amusement – those were what the people needed, or so their leaders thought. Some of them went to great trouble to provide the shows. In 50 B.C., for example, a young aristocrat called Caelius was just beginning his political career, and wanted to win popular support by staging a magnificent Games. So he wrote to his friend Cicero, who was governing the province of Cilicia, and asked him to provide a real novelty, panthers. Cicero's reply, though light-hearted in tone, shows that he did go to a lot of trouble to oblige his young friend, whatever his private feelings about wild-beast shows.

To Cicero, governor, from Caelius, aedile :

Almost every time I write to you I mention panthers. Patiscus has sent Curio ten, and it will look very bad if *you* don't send a lot more. In fact Curio has given those ten to me, along with ten others from Africa – it's

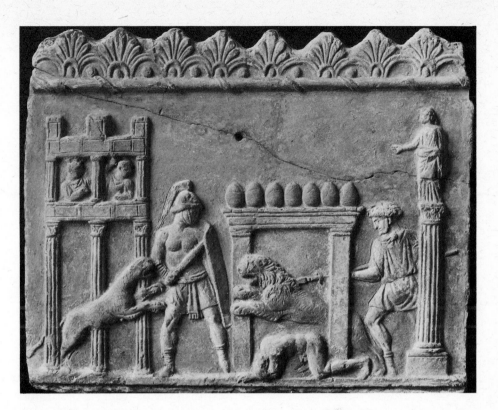

Bestiarii *(fighters of wild beasts), shown in action against a lion and a panther.*

not only country estates he gives away. Please don't forget: send for hunters from Cibyra, and write to Pamphylia (where they say any number of panthers can be caught). That will get things moving.

The reason I'm so concerned *now*, is that it looks as though I'll have to put the whole show on myself, without any help from my colleague. I know you're usually as hard-working as I'm lazy – but please make an extra special effort this time. There's really hardly anything for you to do: a few words, an order or two, and that'll be that.[16]

The answer:

On the subject of panthers: the professional hunters are working flat out, on my instructions. But there's an incredible shortage of panthers; and those that *are* around keep complaining that nothing is ever hunted in the whole province but them. They're moving out, they say, and emigrating to Caria. Nevertheless, we *are* trying hard, especially Patiscus. Any panthers there are will be yours – it's only the number that's in doubt.[17]

Probably what worried aristocrats most about the plebeians was that they were 'politically unstable', and opposed to the conservative style of ruling favoured by the great families. The historian Sallust, writing of the conspiracy organised (with popular support) by the nobleman Catiline in 63 B.C., has this to say about the state of affairs in Rome at the time:

It was then, I think, that the greatness of Rome was at its lowest ebb. Although the whole world, from east to west, had been conquered by our people, and obeyed them, and although in Rome itself there was peace and prosperity (which men think more important than anything else), none the less there were still some citizens determined to destroy both themselves and their state.

And it wasn't only the conspirators who were affected in this way: without exception the common people (who always favour change) supported what Catiline was doing. This is entirely typical. In any state those who have nothing envy those who have plenty, despise tradition, praise evil men and follow the latest fashion; because they can't bear their own lives, they insist that *everything* must be changed.[18]

Almost all that's written about ordinary people is as critical and contemptuous as that. Fortunately, however, artists and sculptors were not as prejudiced as writers (perhaps because fewer of them were from the upper classes). From them we can see that the plebeians didn't spend *every* minute of the day gaping at the Games or plotting revolutions:

Etruscan fishermen.

Right: *Buying cushions.*

Below: *A knife-shop.*

A carpenter working on a ship.

6 · The women of Rome

Roman society was carefully organised. Everyone knew his place, and was expected to keep to it. This was especially true of women – the consul speaks:

It was with considerable embarrassment that I made my way here to the forum just now, through a great crowd of women. I respect each one of them individually as her dignity and honour demands – and it's respect I don't feel at all for them in the mass. This respect is all that prevented me from saying to them, with full consular authority, 'What's the matter? What's brought you out in public like this, blocking the streets, talking to

A butcher's shop. The women are shop-workers: no rich lady would handle meat for herself.

An ivory carving of a Roman lady sacrificing, helped by a slave.

men not related to you? Couldn't each of you have asked your husbands the same questions at home, in private? Do you feel you have more charm in the streets than in your own homes, and with other men than with your own husbands? In any case, if you stayed at home and minded the proper business of women, you wouldn't be remotely interested in what laws were passed or repealed in this assembly.'[1]

Those remarks date from 195 B.C., and it may seem that things were bound to improve. But this comment, from a writer of 300 years later, shows that Roman men, conquerors of the world or not, still hankered after their old caveman ways:

Once our women were pure, and free from vice. Poverty saw to that: poor homes, hard work, too little sleep, hands rough from spinning wool, while Hannibal threatened Rome, and their menfolk guarded the city gates. But now we endure the miseries of eternal peace: luxury, a cancer worse than war, has settled here and punishes us for conquering the world.[2]

To help keep women in their place, savage laws – like this one – were passed in the 'good old days' of these extracts:

If you catch your wife with another man, you can put her to death without trial, and no one will question your right to do so. But if you commit adultery yourself, your wife can't touch you for it, and has no legal right to do so.[3]

A similar attitude is shown in the following letter, about a bereaved husband:

Our friend Macrinus has suffered a terrible blow: he has lost a wife whose qualities would have been outstanding even in the olden days. He lived with her for thirty-nine years without a single quarrel or argument. She always treated him with the greatest respect, and deserved as much respect herself. She seemed to have gathered and stored up in her own character all the good qualities from each stage of a woman's life. Macrinus' greatest consolation, in fact, is that he was able to keep such a treasure for so long; though this fact also makes his loss harder to bear. The greater the pleasure, the more one grieves at losing it. That's why I shall be full

A virtuous old lady.

of concern for my dear friend until he submits to treatment and allows his wound to heal – and the best medicines for this are sheer necessity, the passing of time, and the feeling that you have grieved enough.[4]

The wife is hardly talked of at all, except as someone who reflected credit on her husband – much as an honest slave or a faithful dog might have done. In another letter the same writer, the lawyer Pliny, gives this description of his own wife, whom he married when he was over forty and she was sixteen:

My wife is sensible and a good housekeeper: she loves me – and that's a sure proof of her virtue! Her affection for me has even led her to take an interest in literature. She has copies of all my works, constantly reads them and even learns parts of them by heart. How concerned she is when I have a case on hand, how relieved when it is finished! She has servants waiting in court to tell her what effect I'm making, how much applause I get, and whether I win the case or lose it. Then again, if I'm giving a recitation, she sits in an alcove screened by a curtain, and hears every word of praise with eager delight. She has even set some of my poems to music, and sings them to lute accompaniment – and she's had no music teacher but love, the best of all instructors.[5]

Of course, marriages weren't always as idyllic as that, for the husband at least. No woman of spirit, even if she deferred to her husband in public, would be likely to keep quiet in private *all* the time. As the satirist Juvenal said:

A bed with a wife in it is full of fighting and arguing: no hope at all of sleep. She moans at her husband there, worse than a tigress howling for her lost cubs – as if nagging *him* was going to cure her own guilty conscience.[6]

Martial agreed:

Why doesn't Afer 'rest his weary head'?
The answer's easy: look who shares his bed.[7]

When things were as bad as that, there were two solutions available: adultery and divorce. Divorce was very easy: you handed your wife back her dowry, and returned her to her own family. Many aristocrats used it frequently – even the emperor Augustus, a fervent moral reformer:

When he was young, he was engaged to the daughter of Publius Servilius Isauricus; but when he first quarrelled with Mark Antony and then made it up again, the soldiers on both sides insisted that they should be united by family ties as well, so he married Antony's step-daughter Claudia, the daughter of Antony's wife Fulvia and her first husband Publius Clodius. This girl was hardly even old enough to marry; and Augustus soon quarrelled with his mother-in-law Fulvia, and divorced Claudia before the marriage was consummated. Then he married Scribonia; she had had two previous husbands, both gentlemen of the highest rank, and had a child by the second of them. Augustus divorced her as well, writing that he was sick of her easy-going morals. Immediately afterwards he took Livia Drusilla away from her husband Tiberius Nero, despite the fact that she was pregnant at the time. She was the one woman he really loved: he stayed with her for the rest of his life.[8]

The other alternative, adultery, was even easier. Some writers – Ovid, for example – devoted whole books to the subject of how to find the ideal mistress, and how to set about courting her:

Go to the Circus, where fine horses race:
A crowded Circus is a splendid place
For courtship – no need here for caution, no
Need here to nod or keep your voices low.
You fancy her? Well, sit beside her! Who
Will stop you? Squeeze up close beside her, too.
'I'm sorry, am I squashing you? This rail's
Too close, I've got no room here.' – never fails.
The Games begin, the ice is broken – make
Your first moves carefully: your love's at stake.
'Which riders do you fancy? X and Y?
Now isn't that amazing? So do I!
Oh look, they've started the procession. How
I love those statues! (Venus, help me now!)
Good heavens! On your breast, a speck of sand –

A chariot race in full swing. With all this to watch, it's surprising that Ovid's attention wandered.

Just let me brush it off for you – by hand.'
There isn't any sand? So what? Pretend,
You fool, and brush it just the same. A blend
Of cheek and luck, that's what you need: so play
With care, use all the chances sent your way.
'Oh look, your cloak's been trailing in the dust!
I'll pick it up for you . . . that's better . . . just
A little higher . . . there!' You'll get your prize:
A pair of legs to feast your hungry eyes.
Say sharply to the people sat behind,
'You're kicking her! Be careful! Do you mind?'
Girls' minds are simple, easy to attract:
You'll win her heart with cushions – that's a fact.
No cushions? Fan her with your programme, then,
Or offer her your footstool. Many men
Have found the Circus makes seduction flower
As though the sand itself had magic power.[9]

And some of the most beautiful of all love-poems are those written by Catullus to his mistress, whom he calls Lesbia:

Dancing-girls (all slaves).

You ask, my Lesbia, how many kisses
Will satisfy my love? Count up the grains
Of desert sand in African Cyrene,
Where incense grows; count every grain,
From the oracle of sweltering Ammon
To the holy shrine of ancient Battus;
Then count up the stars by night that see
Our scurrying earth-bound love-affairs;
Then for each grain of sand, each star, one kiss –
Till I am drunk with kisses none can count
Or wish away in tongue-tied jealousy.[10]

Later on their affair turned sour, and ended in bitterness and anger.
The fault seems to have been that Lesbia, like many women of her
day, was easily bored and always on the lookout for new amusement,
new lovers, new excitements. Women like her are described by
Sallust, when he is discussing the women who joined the conspiracy
of Catiline; this lady, called Sempronia, is typical of them all:

The mistress prepares to face the world.

At that time he is said to have recruited large numbers of men of all kinds, and also quite a few women who had in the past paid for their extravagant way of life by prostitution; then, when increasing age ended this source of income without lessening their expensive tastes, they had got deeply into debt. Catiline hoped to use these women in Rome, to stir up the slaves, set the city ablaze, and make their husbands support him, or else kill them.

One of these women was called Sempronia. In the past she had often behaved with a boldness and daring more usual in a man. She was beautiful and of good family, and her husband and children gave her no cause for complaint. She had studied Latin and Greek literature, could play the lute, and dance more skilfully than a decent woman ought; she had many other qualities too, of the sort that go with expensive tastes. But she had never thought anything at all of honour and reputation; she squandered her good name as recklessly as her money, and was so lustful and passionate that *she* pursued men, not the other way round. Before meeting Catiline she had already broken promises, betrayed trusts, been an accessory to murder, and plunged headlong down the path to extravagance and ruin. None the less she was no fool: she wrote poetry,

A slave girl decanting perfume.

was witty, could converse with decency, modesty or coarseness, as the occasion demanded – in fact, she was in many ways an attractive and charming woman.[11]

Women without Sempronia's natural advantages had to make do with other means of making themselves attractive. There was plenty of advice available, too – most of it, of course, written by men. Artificial beauty-aids were particularly favoured. Here, for example, is one of Ovid's recipes for makeup:

When sleep deserts your gentle limbs, arise
And learn the way to dazzle all men's eyes.
First take some barley, which (as you will note)
Our Libyan colonists send here by boat;
Remove the stalks and husks, till 2 pounds' weight
Of grain is left. Break 10 eggs on a plate,
And soak with them the same amount of vetch.
Next, dry your barley in the wind, and fetch
A lumbering ass to grind it into flour.
Then wait until the young stag's finest hour,
And when his budding horns begin to swell
And moult, collect 2 ounces; powder well,
Add all the other dry ingredients,
And sieve them up together. Next, the scents:
Take 12 narcissus-bulbs, skin them with care
And grind them up on marble; then prepare
2 ounces of Etruscan gum, and honey –
9 times the total weight, to make it runny.
Whoever puts this mixture on her face
Will make her looking-glass take second place.[12]

Other writers disapprove strongly of women wasting time, effort and money trying to improve their appearance. These comments on hair-dressing are by Tertullian, one of the early Christian Fathers. The photos show the sort of thing he is describing.

All this wasted pains on arranging your hair – what contribution can this make to your salvation? Why can't you give it a rest? One minute you're

Elaborate hair-style of the first century A.D.

A young noblewoman: the ideal wife personified.

building it up, the next letting it down; raising it one minute, stretching it the next. Some women devote all their energy to forcing their hair to curl, others to making it straight, or hanging loose and wavy in a style which may seem natural, but isn't natural at all. You perpetrate unbelievable extravagances to make a kind of tapestry of your hair, sometimes to be a sort of sheath to your head and a lid to the top of you, like a helmet, sometimes to be an elevated platform, built up on the back of your neck.[13]

It's hardly surprising – if this is how Roman men viewed their women – that, as Cicero says:

Our ancestors decreed that all women, being somewhat short of common sense, should be kept under the power of guardians.[14]

But there is another side to the picture. If Roman women had all been as bad as moral or satirical writers – all male – suggest, they would never have had the power and authority they did in fact possess. Not publicly – for no lady ever took part in public life if she could avoid it – but in private. A famous epitaph on a Roman lady says simply, 'She kept house; she saw to the wool'. The household was left almost entirely under the wife's control, and she and her slaves saw to the education of children below the age of seven – the most formative years of their lives.

Roman history is full of the names of women who honoured their sex: the Sabine Women, whose story is told in Chapter 7; Arria the wife of Paetus; Brutus' wife Portia; the empresses Livia and Agrippina; and perhaps the most famous of all, Coriolanus' mother Veturia and wife Volumnia. Their story dates from long before the dismissive speech quoted at the start of this chapter; it shows not only that some Roman women had character, but that their menfolk recognised it and praised them for it. Certainly Coriolanus' mother and wife, for centuries afterwards, were quoted admiringly as examples of all those qualities that had made Rome great.

Coriolanus, the great Roman general, had for various reasons been exiled, and had gone to join the enemy, the Volsci, who made him their leader. His troops were threatening Rome itself; the Senate didn't know what to do, and the people were in an ugly mood.

Livia and Augustus: the 'ideal' marriage.

The consuls were now Spurius Nautius and Sextus Furius. While they were gathering troops and setting up sentry-posts on the walls and the other places they'd decided should be patrolled and guarded, a huge crowd gathered, demanding peace. Terrified by the hostile attitude of these people, the consuls had no choice but to call a meeting of the Senate and arrange for messengers to go and ask Coriolanus to end the war.

The Senate, seeing how much the people's courage had shrunk, agreed to the proposal; messengers were sent to Coriolanus, and asked for peace. But this was the unbending answer they brought back: 'If you give the Volsci back their land, peace-negotiations can begin; but so long as you do nothing but enjoy what you have stolen, I shall forget neither the injustice of my fellow-citizens nor the kindness of my enemies, and I shall show you clearly that exile has sharpened my spirits, not depressed them.'

The messengers were sent again to Coriolanus, but this time weren't allowed into his camp. One account says that priests even went to the enemy camp in full regalia, to beg for peace; but they had as little effect on Coriolanus as the ambassadors had done.

Then the women of Roman came in large numbers to Veturia, Coriolanus' mother, and to his wife Volumnia. Whether this was state policy, or merely the result of the women's fear, I don't know; but whatever the reason, they succeeded in persuading Veturia (a very old woman) and Volumnia to go to the enemy camp, taking with them Coriolanus' two

Portrait-bust of a young wife.

sons – they hoped that women's prayers and tears might save a city which men had failed to protect, for all their arms and armour.

When they arrived at the camp, Coriolanus was informed that a large group of women was at hand. His immediate response – as you'd expect from a man who cared nothing for the honour due to ambassadors, and as little for the power of religion paraded before him by the priests – was that he would not be moved by women's tears. But then one of his friends, who had recognised Veturia standing beside her daughter-in-law and grandsons, marked out from the rest by her grief, said, 'Unless my eyes deceive me, your mother, wife and sons are here as well.'

Coriolanus, almost beside himself, jumped up at once, and as his mother approached, went to kiss her. But she, abandoning prayers for anger, said, 'Wait! Before you kiss me, I must know whether it's to my son that I've come, or to an enemy. Am I your prisoner or your mother? To think that this is all my long life and unhappy old age have brought me – my son first an exile, then an enemy. How could you bear to devastate this land, which bore you and brought you up? Why did the anger and fury not leave your heart as soon as you crossed our frontiers? When you came in sight of Rome, did you not reflect, "Inside these battlements are my birthplace, my home, my mother, my wife, my children?" I see that if I'd never borne a son, Rome would not now be threatened; if I'd had no son I'd have died a free woman, in a free state. But now I at least can suffer nothing more shameful, or shaming to you; and I will not have long

Roman womanhood deified: the city of Antioch, shown as the goddess Fortune enthroned; Augustus and Livia enthroned, with figures showing the achievements of their family, their children and the gods who favoured them.

to live in such misery. No, it's these others you must consider: if you persist, they'll have nothing ahead of them but an untimely death or a lifetime of slavery.'

When she'd finished, Coriolanus' wife and sons embraced him, and the women's weeping, both for themselves and their country, at last broke the man's spirit. He kissed his family, and sent them home; then he moved his camp back from the city walls. Once his army had gone from Roman soil, it's not clear how he died: some say from shame at what had happened, others in other ways. Fabius, the oldest authority I can find, says that Coriolanus lived to a ripe old age; at any rate (adds Fabius) he often said that exile is even more unbearable when you're old.

The men of Rome didn't begrudge the women the glory they'd earned – life was much freer of envy in those days. In order to make some permanent memorial, they built and consecrated a temple to Fortuna Muliebris, the goddess who guards the fate of women.[15]

7 · Mistress of the world

Other men, no doubt, shall surpass you in casting bronze, in carving live features from a block of marble; they shall plead better in the law-courts and be able to trace with compasses the movements of the heavens and to describe the rising of the stars. You, man of Rome, remember that your skill shall be to rule nations, to make peace and crown it with law, to spare the humbled and to crush the proud.[1]

This description of Rome's purpose on earth is by the poet Virgil; it is spoken by Aeneas' father, as he stands in the underworld, pointing out to his son the spirits of men who will one day bring fame to the city. Although not written in official language, it may reasonably be taken as the official view of Rome's mission under the emperor Augustus. We shall see that not everyone agreed with it.

But how did the Roman empire start? After the foundation of Rome, this was the next step:

Rome was now strong enough to stand up to any of the neighbouring states, but this situation looked as though it would last for only one generation, because of the scarcity of women. There were not enough in Rome to keep the population at its present level, and there was so far no intermarriage with nearby communities. On the advice of their senators, Romulus then sent round these communities asking for alliances and rights of intermarriage for his newly founded city . . .

His requests got a cool reception everywhere. Partly it was contempt, but partly fear of what this powerful and growing city might mean for them and their descendants. Often the messengers were turned away with such questions as 'Have you opened your gates to female criminals as well? You could make plenty of good matches then!' This sort of remark did not exactly please the young men of Rome and clearly violence was in the air.

Romulus decided that, if there was to be violence, it should be at a time and place of his own choosing, so he pretended not to mind these insults and began to prepare for the Games in honour of Neptune the god of horses. He publicised them in all the neighbouring towns and the Romans used all the resources of those days to make the event memorable and to help spread the word.

A huge crowd came, partly out of curiosity to see what this new town was like. Most of them were from near by, from Genina, Crustumium and Antemnae, and also the whole population of Sabinum, including wives and children. The Romans invited them into their homes and when they'd inspected the lay-out of the city and fortifications and saw how many houses there were, they were amazed that so much had been done in such a short time. The hour for the show arrived and all eyes and minds were fully occupied. This was the moment the Romans had chosen for their display of violence; at a signal, the young Romans dashed into the crowd and seized the young women. Mostly the girls were taken by whoever came across them first, but some of the more beautiful ones had been earmarked for leading senators and were carried off to their houses by specially recruited gangs . . .

The festival broke up in a panic and the girls' parents rushed away distraught, complaining that the right of hospitality had been broken and calling on Neptune, to whose festival they had come in trust, only to be deceived. The girls, too, were as anguished about their future and just as indignant, but Romulus went round and spoke to them:

'The fault', he said, 'is in your fathers' pride, which prompted them to stop you intermarrying with us. But now you are married and you will share in all the benefits and privileges of Rome; and, what is more, you will share in the greatest blessing of the human race – children. Let your anger die, and let your hearts follow your bodies into captivity. Indignation often gives way to love. And your husbands, I know, will treat you well. They see it as their duty not only to be your husbands, but to take the place of the parents you have lost.' Their husbands helped with flattering speeches, saying they'd only behaved like that because they were so much in love. No woman can resist appeals of that sort.[2]

Like the stories of Romulus and Horatius, this is myth rather than history, but it probably does represent some local treaty, reached after a period of warfare. Local wars occupied the Romans until

Neptune, god of horses and the sea, in whose honour the Sabine women came to Rome.

A coin of 88 B.C. showing Romulus ('heads') and the Rape of the Sabines ('tails').

early in the third century B.C., when they ventured first into north Greece, and then into north Africa for the first war against Carthage. This was indecisive, and both sides re-armed for a bigger encounter:

I'd like to state at this point, as many historians have done right at the beginning of their works, that I'm now going to write about the most memorable war in history. The two nations concerned were stronger than any others before them, and were both at the peak of their own prosperity and power. They had each learnt, in the First Punic War, what to expect from their opponent and when it came the struggle was so even (the advantage going first one way, then the other), that the eventual winners were the ones who had come nearer to defeat.[3]

After sixteen years of fighting, the Romans won (see Chapter 4), and gained confidence and the beginnings of an empire. Their next campaigns were to 'liberate' oppressed peoples in Greece:

The Romans took their places for the games and the herald stepped forwards, as usual, with a trumpeter into the middle of the arena. The games are always opened from this place with a ritual chant and now a fanfare on the trumpet obtained silence. The herald read out his announcement:
    'The Roman Senate and T. Quinctius their general, having conquered King Philip and the Macedonians, declare that the Corinthians, the Phocians, all the Locrians, the island of Euboea, the Magnesians, the Thessalians, the Perrhaebians and the Achaeans of Phthiotis shall be free, shall not pay tribute, and shall be governed by their own laws.' This list included all the states once ruled by King Philip.
    The herald finished his announcement, but the feeling of joy was too great for the audience to realise what it meant to them. They could hardly believe they'd heard correctly, but gazed round at one another dumbfounded, as though they'd seen a ghost. Not trusting their own ears, they asked their neighbours how the announcement would affect themselves. The herald was called back again, as they wanted to see as well as hear the voice of their freedom, and made his announcement once more. This time there was no doubt. The shouts and the applause went on and on. Anyone could see that of all the things the people wanted, what they wanted most was freedom.[4]

Corinth, after it had been 'liberated' by the Romans.

Fine words: Twenty-seven years later, and only some 240 kilometres farther north:

Paullus called for ten leading men from each city, and told them to have the gold and silver brought out into the public squares. Then he sent cohorts to all the cities, staggering their departure times, so that they would all reach their destinations at the same moment. The tribunes and centurions had received their orders; early in the morning all the gold and silver was collected and at 10 o'clock the soldiers were given the signal to ransack the cities. There was plenty for the taking. Each cavalryman had a share amounting to 1,600 sesterces and each infantryman 800, while 150,000 human beings were led off into slavery. When the plundering was finished, the city walls were smashed down. The cities involved numbered around seventy.[5]

This was not an isolated example, either. After the provinces were won, Rome put in governors to rule them. We can see the size of the military forces stationed in some of these provinces from remains of

Timgad, in Algeria. This town, built for retired soldiers, also served as a showplace, to impress the natives with Roman power and magnificence.

the buildings put up to house them. For example, Timgad, in north Africa, was founded by Trajan as a settlement to which veteran soldiers could retire. With such forces behind them, provincial governors were hard men to resist, when they saw the road to instant wealth open in front of them:

When you finally get your province, don't give way entirely to fury and greed. Spare a thought for the poor locals – you'll find their bones sucked dry of marrow – and stick to the law and the Senate's instructions, think what the rewards are for those who govern honestly and remember the thunderbolt the Senate justly aimed at Capito and Numitor, the two wreckers of Cilicia . . .

Maybe you despise the feeble Rhodians and the Corinthians drenched in perfume – well, who's to blame you! Scented young men with shaved legs wouldn't cause you much trouble. But steer clear of Spain, it's tough; and keep away from Gaul and the coast of Illyria. And give those African peasants a miss, sweating away to feed a Rome which is only interested in horses and actors. Not that you'd get much if you tried – it's not long since Marius Priscus stripped them to the bone. The main thing is not to have a go at brave men who have nothing to lose. You can take away all their gold and silver, but they'll still have their shields and swords and javelins and helmets.[6]

More straightforward is Cicero's advice to his younger brother, out in a province of Asia Minor:

You have among your staff men you can praise when they do their duty, or very easily call to order when they are lax about obeying your instructions. When you were new to the job, it seems these men were able to impose on your good nature; the better we are, the more difficult it is to suspect evil in others. But now you're entering your third year of office. Show yourself as honest as before, but still more wary and hard-working. Let it be known that your ears hear only what is plainly spoken and are not open to lies and inventions whispered to make a profit. Your signet-ring should not be just a tool of the trade, but almost a duplicate of you yourself; that's to say, not a servant to anyone else's will, but the witness of your own.

Your orderly should be the sort intended by our ancestors. They regarded his job, not as a soft option, but as a post involving hard work and responsibility, and preferred to fill it from their own freedmen, whom they could control almost as completely as slaves. Your lictor should dispense not his own mercy, but yours, and the insignia he carries should be more symbols of office than of real power. In short, see that the whole province realises how much you care for the safety, the children, the

Trajan, the soldier-emperor from Spain.

reputation and the fortunes of all those under your control. Finally, make sure that not only the takers but also the givers of bribes know that, if you find them out, you'll be no friend of theirs. Indeed, bribery will cease when they realise they can get nothing out of you by relying on men who boast that you are in their pocket . . . It seems to me there is one touchstone for all those who govern other people: the greatest happiness of their subjects.[7]

Basically, the problem was one of distance. Two months might go by between sending a letter from Rome to Asia Minor and getting a reply. And for the Roman Senate governors were not by any means the only trouble. There were pirates, who before Pompey smashed their organisation in 67 B.C., had roamed the Mediterranean for years. Cicero angrily addresses the Senate:

What province did you keep free from pirates during those years? What revenue could you rely on? What ally could you support? Whom did your navy defend? How many islands do you reckon were deserted and how many allied cities abandoned through fear or capture by pirates?

But why do I recall events so far from home . . . ? Why mention that during those years the sea was closed to our allies, when our own armies could cross from Brundisium only in the depths of winter . . . ? Have you really forgotten that the famous port of Caieta was ransacked by pirates while full of shipping, under the eyes of a praetor? Or that the pirates abducted from Misenum the children of the very man who had just been fighting them there? Must I bring up that terrible affair at Ostia, that black cloud of shame over our city, when, almost before your own eyes, the fleet entrusted to the consul by the people of Rome, was captured by pirates and destroyed?[8]

Then there were the off-beat religious cults – Pliny the Younger, in Asia Minor, writes to the emperor Trajan in Rome around A.D. 112:

I am in the habit of asking your advice, Sir, when I am not sure what action to take, as you are the best person to settle my doubts and provide me with the right information.

I have never until now taken part in questioning Christians, and so I don't know what the punishments usually are or how far to go in pursuing

A war-galley. At the front is the 'beak', for ramming enemy ships below the water-line.

my investigations . . . Various points have given me trouble: should the young be treated more leniently than the adults; if they repent, should they be pardoned, or is it enough to condemn them that they have been Christians once; and is the name 'Christian' itself punishable, or only when accompanied by recognisable offences?

So far, this is how I have dealt with people who were brought to me for being Christians. I ask them if they are Christians: if they admit it, I ask them twice more, and warn them what the punishment is: if they persist

Christians at Mass.

I order them to be executed. I am firmly convinced that, whatever they confess to, such stubbornness and obstinacy deserve to be punished. There have been other fanatics of the same sort, but as they are Roman citizens I have decided that they should be sent to Rome.

As so often happens, now that I have begun to deal with the matter, more and more names are reaching me of people charged with this offence. An anonymous pamphlet is going the rounds with a long list of names on it. Of these, I decided to acquit the ones who said they weren't and never had been Christians, after I had seen them pray to the gods and offer wine and incense to your statue (I had this and statues of the gods brought in specially). They also cursed the name of Christ, and I'm told that no true Christian can be made to do that.

Other names were given to me by an informer. These people first said they were Christians and then changed their minds; they had been, they said, but had given it up three years earlier, or more, and in some cases as much as twenty years earlier. All of these, too, prayed to your statue and those of the gods and cursed the name of Christ. The worst crime they would admit to was that they used to meet on a particular day before dawn and sing, in turn, verses of a hymn to Christ, as though he was a god. They hadn't sworn to commit crime of any sort, but indeed not to steal or rob or commit adultery, not to break their promises or refuse to give back money they'd been lent. Then they'd dispersed, but came back later and had a meal together, consisting of quite ordinary, harmless food. They gave up this last habit after my announcement, which you told me to make, that all political societies were banned. Because of this, I decided I ought to extract the truth, even under torture, from two slave-girls, called 'deaconesses'. All the evidence I got pointed merely to a superstitious cult that had gone too far.

So I have put a temporary stop to questioning and now write urgently to you for advice. The whole business, it seems to me, needs your attention, as there are so many people at risk: all ages and classes, both men and women, are coming before me and will go on doing so. It is not only in the towns either. This religious mania has spread through the villages and the countryside as well. I think, though, that it can be stopped and cured. Certainly, the sacred Roman rites are going through a revival and our temples, which had been empty for years, are now full of people. Everywhere you go the flesh of sacrificial victims is up for sale, and until recently there were no buyers to be found. So it is fair to assume that, if we give these Christians a chance to repent, a large number of people could be brought back on to the right path.

Trajan replies:

You have acted quite properly, my dear Pliny, in the way you have questioned the people brought to you as being Christians. Obviously it is not possible to lay down strict rules to deal with every case, but certainly the Christians must not be hunted down. But if they are brought to you and found guilty, then they must be punished, with this exception: if anyone denies he is a Christian, and makes this fact quite clear by praying to the Roman gods, he must be pardoned, whatever his previous record may be. As to anonymous leaflets, you must certainly not use them as evidence. This kind of thing sets a very bad example and does not fit the image of modern Rome.[9]

Rioting, too, was always a danger. Claudius writes to the Greek section of the multi-racial population of Alexandria:

As to who was responsible for the disturbance and quarrelling (or, to call a spade a spade, war) between you and the Jews, although your

A coin of Claudius' time. This portrait of the emperor is probably more life-like than the statue on page 92.

spokesmen, and Dionysius son of Theon in particular, put up a good showing against their opposite numbers, even so I decided not to go into the matter too closely. But I have stored away inside me a fund of implacable anger against anyone who starts the trouble again. And I tell you plainly, if you don't put a stop to this persistent troublemaking and quarrelling, I shall be forced to show you to what lengths a kind master can go when pressed.

So once more I beg you, men of Alexandria, to treat the Jews in a kind and civilised manner; they have, after all, lived in your city for many years. Also you must not interfere with their religious ceremonies, but let them observe the customs they did under the divine Augustus; I too have given my permission for these to continue, after hearing both sides of the case. On the other hand, I must order the Jews not to agitate for more rights than they had before, and not ever again to send to me a separate embassy as though they had a city of their own. There is absolutely no precedent for this behaviour.

But if both of you will agree to treat each other with tolerance and forbearance, I for my part will take every step to protect your city, remembering the long-standing ties of friendship that bind you to us.[10]

Tolerance was clearly a necessary quality for an emperor. Any tactless display of force might have brought to the boil the simmering hatred towards Rome which certainly existed. The writer Sallust included in his 'Histories' this imaginary letter from Mithridates, King of Pontus to the King of Parthia, on the far side of the Caspian Sea:

There is only one reason, and an ancient one, why the Romans go to war with all nations, peoples and kings – a profound passion for power and riches . . . I am well aware that you have large quantities of men and money; that's why I want your friendship and that's why the Romans want your property . . . Surely you must know that the Romans only turned eastwards to us after their westward progress had been halted by the Atlantic? And from the beginning of their history, what have they possessed except what they have stolen – their homes, their wives, their lands, their empire? Once they were vagabonds without homes or parents. They were put on earth to be a plague to mankind; no laws of god or man can stop them from laying their hands on allies and friends, whether near

Mithridates, appearing as Hercules in his lion-skin cape.

Right: *The sack of Jerusalem. 'Whoever does not bow to Rome . . . is her enemy.'*

or far away, whether weak or powerful, and destroying them. Everything which does not bow to them, and monarchical regimes in particular, is their enemy.[11]

Even if the letter was imaginary, the sentiments were real and held by many of Rome's subjects. Some emperors, such as Augustus and Hadrian, were happy to consolidate what was already conquered. Augustus, in particular, was concerned more with the quality of the empire than its size:

He thought it was very important to keep the Roman people free of any taint of foreign or slavish blood. He was very sparing in his gifts of citizenship and laid down limits for the age and number of slaves who could be set free. When Tiberius asked him to grant citizenship to one of

Tiberius enthroned, on a coin of his own time.

his Greek clients, Augustus replied that the man must come and see him personally and prove that he deserved the honour. His wife Livia made the same request for a Gaul, from a province that paid tax to Rome: Augustus refused it and instead exempted the man from taxes. 'I would rather', he said, 'lose whatever taxes he owes than turn the Roman citizenship into something cheap.'[12]

Augustus' concern for quality paid off. In the forty-five years between his victory over Antony and Cleopatra in 31 B.C. and his death in A.D. 14, he gave Rome the peace she needed after the horrors of civil war. Here is part of his own summary of his life's work:

Our forefathers intended that the gates of the temple of Janus Quirinus should be closed whenever our victories brought peace to the whole Roman empire on land and sea. Although it is recorded that these gates were closed only twice between the foundation of Rome and my own birth, while I was consul the Senate three times gave orders that they were to be shut.[13]

Following generations refused to take Augustus quite as seriously as he took himself. This parody, by an unknown writer, captures his humourless style rather nicely. The scene is Olympus; the gods are discussing the question 'Should Claudius be made a god?':

Then the divine Augustus got up, when it was his turn to speak, and proceeded to talk most eloquently: 'My lords and gentlemen, I call you as witnesses that from the day I became a god I have not made a single speech, I mind my own business. But really I cannot hide my true feelings any longer. My sorrow and, what makes it worse, my shame are too much for me. Was it for this I made peace by land and sea? Was it for this I calmed wars inside the state, gave Rome a firm framework of laws, filled it with beautiful buildings, so that – words fail me, gentlemen: nothing I can say would match my indignation.'[14]

By the time this was written, in the middle of the first century A.D., the purity of the Roman race was a forgotten dream. Freedmen were everywhere:

Well, with the gods on my side I became boss in the house and pulled

Pertinax. Despite the Roman clothing, he is clearly a different physical type from earlier emperors. He ruled for three months.

the wool over my master's eyes. In a word, he made me joint heir with the emperor and I came in for a senator's fortune. But nobody ever has enough. I decided to go into business and, to cut a long story short, I had five ships built, loaded them with wine, which was worth its weight in gold at the time, and sent them off to Rome. Anyone would think I laid the whole thing on: all the ships were sunk – seriously, I'm not joking. In one day Neptune swallowed 30 million sesterces. Do you think I went broke? Good heavens, no! This was nothing, it was just what I needed to get me going. I built some bigger ones, and better and luckier, so no one could say I wasn't a solid fellow – there's nothing like a big ship, you know, for giving a man solidity! I filled them up again with wine, bacon fat, beans, perfume and slaves . . . The gods don't waste time; on one voyage I cleared a round 10 million sesterces, and at once I bought back all the property that had belonged to my patron. I built a house, bought slaves and beasts of burden; everything I touched grew like a honeycomb. When I was worth more than the whole of my home town, I packed it in; I left the business world and started lending money to freedmen . . .

In the meantime, with Mercury behind me, I've built this house. As you know, it was just a shack at one time, but now it's more like a temple. It's got four dining-rooms, twenty bedrooms, two marble colonnades, and upstairs a dining-room, my own bedroom, this bitch's boudoir and a splendid porter's lodge; and I've got room to entertain all my friends.[15]

From the first century A.D., the strains in the class structure developed into a split. The old families died out or lost contact with power, the money was in the hands of freedmen and, at the end of the century, the calm, ordered existence of Rome was threatened by a succession of weak emperors. The third century A.D. was a century of crisis, in which the army got the upper hand; and the army was no longer loyal to Rome but to its own power. Already in A.D. 193 the following scene could take place:

After Pertinax had been killed, Sulpicianus, who was the prefect of Rome and Pertinax's father-in-law, intended to be declared emperor in the camp. Julianus heard that a meeting of the Senate had been called so he arrived at the senate-house with his son-in-law, only to find the doors shut. He found there two tribunes, Publius Florianus and Vectius Aper, and they began urging him to seize power. He pointed out that someone else had

Commodus, the reluctant emperor.

Constantine, who left Rome and ruled from Constantinople (Istanbul).

already been named as emperor, but they grabbed hold of him and took him to the camp. However, when they got there Sulpicianus was holding a meeting and claiming the empire for himself, and nobody would let Julianus in, although he was promising vast amounts of money from outside the wall. Julianus first warned the soldiers not to proclaim as emperor a man who would avenge Pertinax, and wrote on placards that he would restore Commodus to official recognition. So he was let in and proclaimed emperor, although the soldiers asked that Sulpicianus shouldn't suffer for wanting to be emperor himself.[16]

The sense of duty, which had been the guiding force behind Aeneas, behind Horatius, even behind Augustus, was now almost dead. In the fourth century, Constantine transferred control of the eastern empire to Constantinople, and in A.D. 410 the Goths invaded Rome:

Alaric is at the gates, and Rome trembles. He encircles the city; there is panic; he bursts in; but not before giving his instructions, that all those seeking asylum in the holy-places and especially in the churches of the apostles St Peter and St Paul must be left untouched and unharmed. The invading army was also to refrain from bloodshed, while gorging itself on as many valuables as it could find.[17]

The power of Rome was now spiritual rather than material – and has been ever since.

The poet Juvenal wrote of Rome's beginnings:

However far back you insist on tracing your pedigree, it all started from a haven for criminals. Your earliest ancestor, whoever he was, was either a shepherd or something I'd rather not mention.[18]

Even so, only six years after Alaric's invasion, a Roman poet could still write this, echoing our first extract in his idea of the grand, civilising mission of Rome:

O Rome, the world is yours and you its queen;
O Rome, bright star of stars in heav'n above,
Mother of gods and men, hear us, we stand

The goddess Victory, symbol of Roman triumph, lying amid ruins in the African desert.

Within your temples and feel heaven near.
As far as sunlight spreads its gift of life,
Where Ocean's lapping waves enfold the world,
You rule. Through southern sands, through northern snows
The march of Rome went unimpeded on.
Far distant tribes became one fatherland
Beneath your pow'r, which brought to conquered men
The rule of law; and through this common right
You made a city out of all the world.[19]

Chronological chart

CENTURY	AUTHORS AND PRINCIPAL WORKS c. = approximate date	IMPORTANT HISTORICAL EVENTS c. = approximate date
B.C. 800–500		**B.C.** c. 753 Romulus founds Rome 509 Tarquin the Proud (last king) deposed; senatorial government established
400–200	c. 254–184 PLAUTUS (20 surviving comedies) 234–149 CATO (History, Oratory, On Farming)	*Rome colonising in Italy and Mediterranean. Wars with Pyrrhus (280) and Carthaginians (264–202)*
200–100	185–159 TERENCE (6 comedies) 116–27 VARRO (over 600 scientific works; only a few survive, including On Agriculture) 106–43 CICERO (Oratory, Philosophy, Letters) 102–44 CAESAR (Memoirs, The Gallic War and The Civil War)	157–86 Marius, a general and famous military reformer 149–146 Third war against Carthage. Carthage destroyed 146 Destruction of Corinth ends conquest of Greece 138–78 Sulla, dictator of Rome and legal reformer 133–122 Democratic reforms at Rome, lessening aristocratic power 106–48 Pompey, aristocratic general: Caesar's greatest rival
100–0	c. 100–25 NEPOS (History) c. 99–55 LUCRETIUS (The Nature of the Universe) 86–35 SALLUST (History: Catiline and Jugurtha) c. 84–54 CATULLUS (Lyric poetry) 70–19 VIRGIL (Eclogues, Georgics, Aeneid) 65–8 HORACE (Lyric poetry and satire)	73 Revolt of Spartacus 63 Cicero consul; uprising of Catiline 58–51 Caesar conquers Gaul, looks at Britain 49 During Civil War, Caesar invades Italy 44 Caesar assassinated 39 First public library founded in Rome (by Pollio) 27 Augustus becomes first emperor

A.D.			
c. 60–19	TIBULLUS (Love poetry)		
59–A.D. 17	LIVY (History)		
50–A.D. 26	VITRUVIUS (Treatise on architecture)		
c. 50–16	PROPERTIUS (Love poetry)		
43–A.D. 18	OVID (Poetry of many sorts)		
4–A.D. 65	SENECA (Moral and philosophical essays; Letters; 9 tragedies)	c. 3	Jesus Christ born

A.D. 1–100		A.D.	
c. 1–70	VALERIUS (Essayist)	14	Tiberius emperor
34–62	PERSIUS (Satires)	37	Caligula emperor
c. 23–79	PLINY THE ELDER (Scientific writings)	41	Claudius emperor; conquest of Germany and Britain
c. 35–95	QUINTILIAN (*The Training of the Orator*)	54	Nero emperor; persecution of Christians
39–65	LUCAN (Epic poem, *Pharsalia*)	64	Great Fire of Rome
died 65	PETRONIUS (Satire: the *Satyricon*)	68–69	Civil War: 4 emperors
c. 40–104	MARTIAL (Satirical epigrams)	69	Vespasian emperor
c. 40–103	FRONTINUS (Military history)	79	Titus emperor; Pompeii and Herculaneum destroyed by eruption of Vesuvius
c. 55–117	TACITUS (History; treatises on *Germany* and *Oratory*)	81	Domitian emperor
c. 65–140	JUVENAL (16 satires)	96	Nerva emperor
c. 70–160	SUETONIUS (Lives of famous men, including *Twelve Caesars*)	98	Trajan emperor; conquest of Germany and outlying parts of empire completed

100–410			
c. 110–180	GAIUS (Law)	117	Hadrian emperor
c. 120–200	GELLIUS (Essayist and writer of anthologies)		*Between 192 and 306 there were 33 emperors, many of whom were assassinated. Barbarian invasions begin in east and west*
c. 120–180	FRONTO (Rhetoric)		
c. 130–200	APULEIUS (Novel: *The Golden Ass*)		
c. 150–220	FESTUS (Christian writings)		
c. 150–230	TERTULLIAN (Christian writings)	312	Constantine, first Christian emperor
c. 250–320	LACTANTIUS (Christian writings)	330	Constantinople founded; 2 empires (eastern and western)
c. 330–400	AMMIANUS (History)		
c. 240–420	JEROME (Latin translation of Bible)		
354–430	AUGUSTINE (Religious writings)	410	Rome sacked by Alaric
c. 360–420	VEGETIUS (Military history)		
c. 390–460	RUTILIUS (Christian poetry)		
c. 400–470	OROSIUS (History of the world)		

Suggestions for further reading

1. Authors quoted in this book

Detailed references to all the passages quoted can be found on pages 134–5. It is difficult to recommend complete translations of most of the writers, however. In some cases (e.g. Virgil) there is a wealth of choice; in others (e.g. Orosius) practically none. In the case of some of the verse-writers (Horace, Martial and Juvenal in particular) no current translation really gives an accurate impression at all.

The following authors will be found in whole or in part in the Penguin Classics series: Apuleius, Caesar, Catullus, Cicero, Horace, Juvenal, Livy, Lucan, Lucretius, Ovid, Petronius, Plautus, Pliny the Younger, Sallust, Seneca, Suetonius, Tacitus and Virgil. For the others, the Loeb Classical Library (Macmillan) offers bilingual editions, the Latin text facing a rather antiquated translation. The Dell Company of America has published paperback translations of many of the standard Latin authors, and a few unusual ones as well.

In general, however, it is better (in our opinion) to look around in bookshops for oneself – in Latin authors, as in no others, one man's meaty translation is so often another's poison. Much of the work of minor writers has been anthologised: the *Penguin Book of Latin Verse in Translation* and Helen Waddell's *Medieval Latin Lyrics* are outstanding examples. Many of the obscurer writers quoted in this book can be found, in fuller detail, in Lewis and Reinhold's two-volume collection of Latin historical writings, *Roman Civilisation* (Harper and Rowe).

2. General reading

P. D. Arnott, *Introduction to the Roman World* (Macmillan).
   A good general introduction, with useful photographs.
Marcel Brion, *Pompeii and Herculaneum* (Elek Books).
Barry Cunliffe, *Fishbourne* (Phaidon).
   Beautifully illustrated archaeological books.
Michael Grant, *The World of Rome* (Cardinal); *The Climax of Rome* (Weidenfeld and Nicolson); *Gladiators* (Penguin); *Julius Caesar* (Panther); *Nero* (Corgi); *The Roman Forum* (Weidenfeld and Nicolson); *Cities of Vesuvius* (Weidenfeld and Nicolson).

Any book with Dr Grant's name on it will interest and intrigue both the specialist and the ordinary reader.

Gilbert Highet, *Poets in a Landscape* (Hamish Hamilton).
A superb book, full of scholarliness, fine translations, beautiful photos.

J. Maclean-Todd, *Voices from the Past* (Macmillan).
An anthology containing the best bits of almost every Greek and Latin author of importance, in usually very good translations.

H. H. Scullard and Van Der Heyden, *Atlas of the Classical World* (Nelson).
500 photos, maps, diagrams and a good text.

D. E. Strong, *The Classical World* (Hamlyn).
A good picture-book.

Aspects of Roman Life Series (Longman).
Greek and Roman Topics Series (Allen & Unwin).
Inside the Ancient World Series (Macmillan).
Topic books on single subjects, suitable for readers from eleven upwards, 'O' Level, and undergraduate level respectively.

List of passages quoted

1 · The Roman mind

[1] Sallust, *Catiline* LI, 37–9
[2] Horace, *Epistles* II, i, 28–33, 156–7
[3] Pliny, *Natural History* I (de lib. XXXI)
[4] Lucretius I, 50–7
[5] Cato, *De agri cultura* CLVI, i
[6] Martial IV, 32
[7] Suetonius, *Augustus*, LXXII
[8] Pliny, *Epistles* III, 5, iiif. (with some cuts)
[9] Tacitus, *De oratore* XXIX, 1–4
[10] Quintilian I, 1, iv
[11] Pliny, *Epistles* IV, 13, 3–6, 9
[12] Juvenal VII, 215–43
[13] Horace, *Epistles* II, i, 69–75
[14] Quintilian I, praefatio, 9–12
[15] Tacitus, *De oratore* XXXI, 1
[16] Cicero, *In Verrem* II, v, 64, 166, 171
[17] Suetonius, *Caligula* XXXII, 3
[18] Catullus XCIII
[19] Martial IX, 5; XI, 64; XI, 67
[20] Martial V, 34

2 · Myth, magic and religion

[1] Livy I; 3, 4, 6–7 (abridged)
[2] Livy II, 10
[3] Virgil, *Aeneid* IV, 259–84, 331–47, 356–61
[4] Ovid, *Metamorphoses* VI, 339–81
[5] Festus, 82, 11–13
[6] DESSAU 8751 (a), 8753 (b) [I.L.S. II²]
[7] Cato, *De agri cultura*, CLX
[8] Livy VII, 3, 1–4
[9] Aulus Gellius, *Noctes Atticae* I, xii, 1–10
[10] DESSAU 5050, 90–105 [I.L.S. II¹]
[11] Horace, *Carmen Saeculare*, 49–68
[12] Tacitus, *Annals* IV, 37–8
[13] Suetonius, *Caligula*, 33
[14] Suetonius, *Vespasian*, 23
[15] Juvenal VI, 526–34, 539–41
[16] Apuleius, *Metamorphoses* XI, 9–10
[17] Seneca, *Epistles* CIV, 7–10
[18] Tacitus, *Annals* XV, 62, 63, 64, iii–iv
[19] Lactantius, *De mortibus persecutorum*, 36
[20] Augustine, *City of God* V, 17 (abridged)

3 · Town and country

[1] Seneca, *Epistles* LVI, 1–5 (slightly cut)
[2] Juvenal III, 234–48, 254–61
[3] Suetonius, *Nero* XXXI, 1–10
[4] Suetonius, *Nero* XXXVIII, 1–5
[5] Juvenal III, 194–202
[6] Plautus, *Aulularia*, 505–22, 524–31
[7] Juvenal I, 95–106
[8] Martial VI, 88
[9] Table VII, 6, 7, 9, 10 [Loeb *Remains of Old Latin* 424–515]
[10] Cicero *In Verrem* II, 2, 74 §183–75 §185

4 · At war

[1] Livy V, 19–21 (abridged)
[2] Livy I, 43
[3] Livy VIII, 8
[4] Pliny, *Epistles* VII, 22
[5] P. MICH. VIII, 468, 35ff
[6] Vegetius I, 5
[7] COD. THEOD. VII, 13, 3–4
[8] Vegetius I, 9–10 (abridged), 19
[9] Livy XXII, 3–5 (abridged)
[10] Livy XXX, 33–5 (abridged)
[11] Tacitus, *Annals* XIII, 35
[12] Sallust, *Jugurtha*, 85 (abridged)
[13] Valerius Maximus II, 3, 2
[14] Frontinus, *Strat.* IV, 2, 2
[15] Caesar, *B.G.* VII, 72
[16] Suetonius, *Caesar*, 51
[17] Lucan, *Pharsalia* I, 143–50
[18] Loeb, *Select Papyri* (1934), no. 211
[19] Pliny, *Epistles* X, 19, 20
[20] Tacitus, *Agricola* XXX
[21] Horace, *Epode* VII
[22] Cicero, *De officiis* I, xi, 34–5

Also in column 3:
[11] Martial XI, 3
[12] Pliny, *Epistles* I, 13, i
[13] Pliny, *Epistles* VIII, 21, ii–iv
[14] Pliny, *Epistles* I, 9
[15] Pliny, *Epistles* V, 6, vii–xiii
[16] Pliny, *Epistles* II, 17, i–v, xx–xxiv
[17] Virgil, *Georgics* II, 467–74
[18] Cicero, *De officiis* II, 25 (89)
[19] Tibullus II, i, 1–30

5 · Ordinary people

1 Seneca, *Epistles* XLVII, I
2 Cato, *De agri cultura* LVI–LIX
3 Varro, *De agri cultura* I, xviii, 1–2
4 Varro, *De agri cultura* I, xvii, 4–7
5 Pliny, *Epistles* III, 14, i–v
6 Suetonius, *Claudius* 25, v
7 Pliny, *Epistles* VIII, 16, i–ii
8 Plautus, *Pseudolus* 790–838
9 Cicero, *De officiis* I, 42 (slightly cut)
10 Martial VII, 64
11 Suetonius, *Claudius* 28, 29, i–ii
12 Plautus, *Curculio* 288–95
13 Pliny, *Epistles* IX, 6
14 Seneca, *Epistles* VII, 2–5
15 Juvenal X, 72–81
16 Cicero, *Ad familiares* VIII, 9, ii–iii (cut)
17 Cicero, *Ad familiares* II, 11, ii
18 Sallust, *Catiline*, XXXVII 4, XXXVII 3 (cut)

6 · The women of Rome

1 Livy XXXIV, 2, viii–x
2 Juvenal VI, 287–93
3 Aulus Gellius 10, 23, 5
4 Pliny, *Epistles* VIII, 5
5 Pliny, *Epistles* IV, 19, ii–v
6 Juvenal VI, 268–71
7 Martial X, 84
8 Suetonius, *Augustus* 62
9 Ovid, *Ars amatoria* I, 135–64
10 Catullus VII
11 Sallust, *Catiline*, 24 iii–25 v
12 Ovid, *De med. fac.*, 51–68
13 Tertullian, *De cultu feminarum*, 2, 7
14 Cicero, *pro Murena* XII, 27
15 Livy II, 39 ix–40 xii

7 · Mistress of the world

1 Virgil, *Aeneid* VI, 847–53
2 Livy I, 9 (cut)
3 Livy XXI, 1, i–ii (cut)
4 Livy XXXIII, 32, iv–ix
5 Livy XLV, 34, ii–vi
6 Juvenal VIII, 87–94, 112–24
7 Cicero, *Ad Quint* I, 1, xii–xiii, xxiv
8 Cicero, *Pro lege Manilia* XI 32–XII 33 (abridged)
9 Pliny, *Epistles* X, 96, 97
10 Loeb, *Select Papyri* (1934), no. 212 (abridged)
11 Sallust, *Historiarum* IV, 61, v, xvi–xvii (cut)
12 Suetonius, *Augustus* XL, 3
13 *Monumentum Ancyranum*, 13 (in Loeb *Velleius Paterculus etc*)
14 Seneca, *Apocolocyntosis* 10
15 Petronius, *Satyricon* 76–7 (abridged)
16 Hist. Aug. Did. Iul. II, 4–7, III, 2–4
17 Orosius VII, 39, i
18 Juvenal VIII, 272–5
19 Namatianus I, 46–66 (slightly cut)

The forum or main square of Pompeii, seen through one of the city gates. The stone pillars were there to keep out wheeled traffic.